The Screenplay Series

SOPHIA

Sophia

AlbinoPigGorilla Press

For information:
www.meltoncartes.com
www.albinopiggorilla.com

ISBN: 979-8-9943732-8-6

Printed in the United States of America

This screenplay is part of
The Screenplay Series of published screenplays,
in paperback and e-book.

<u>Sophia</u>

an original screenplay

written by

Melton Eduardo Cartes

As Armageddon unfolds, a tormented
priest battling Satan discovers the
apocalypse is an illusion staged by a
hidden figure, forcing him to question
his faith, his reality, and the very
fabric of the universe.

FADE IN:

TITLE CARD: The Universe is made of love.

EXT. PALESTINE - DUSK

Armageddon is happening.

INSERT: CNN and other media fill their screens with horrible and terrifying images of the End of the World occurring in the Middle East. But the reality...

...is far worse.

The combined Arab military forces are in full battle with the Israeli armed forces, beating them down. The focus of the battle is the Negeb desert (the Arabic name), southeast of Gaza that had already been devastated by IDF bombs.

It looks like a huge grey, brown storm cell has formed over the region, swirling smoke, sand, and metaphysics.

IDF planes STREAK by, dropping ordinance. Huge mushroom clouds fill the air. Explosions REVERBERATE across the area.

Missile smoke streaks into the Israeli Arrow, David's Sling, and the Iron Dome, overwhelming those defenses, some explode midair, many others reach their targets.

Artillery, tanks, and infantry FIRE their weapons at will. Tracers cross the space in a spider web of death.

A blonde, blue-eyed warrior runs up on the ruins of a building, GALEN (30, German). His strange suit of armor, a flowing, organic design made of some dark red material, is blood-spattered. It looks poured onto his body and hardened.

He's brandishing a long lance that CRACKLES with energy from the long blade on the end. What can be seen of his neck has a nasty scar, up high.

He looks around desperately and spots a DARK VORTEX ahead, in the center of the battle. He runs toward it.

Other similarly armored warriors follow him. These are not IDF nor Arabs. They represent some other fighting force.

Galen makes his way amidst the weapons fire. His Cohorts fan out as they join him. They are bloodied and exhausted but formidable still.

The Dark Vortex has stopped in what compares to the eye of a tornado; the entire battle rages around all of them.

The center of the Dark Vortex holds a large man. He too wears armor similar to Galen's, but it's more complex, frightening and lethal.

                         GALEN
              STOP!

The Dark Vortex turns and faces Galen. It is a man only in that it has similar features, a face with eyes, nose, and mouth and the rest of the physique of a giant.

Galen aims his staff. His Cohorts do was well.

The Dark Vortex glares and sneers. His skin is a swirl of alabaster and red translucent tones that constantly move. The waves of dark energy waft around him like smoke from a wet fire. It periodically flies off to parts of the battle.

The Cohorts spread out, surrounding the Dark Vortex. He raises his hands and black waves of energy spew out.

                    GALEN (CONT'D)
          You have nowhere to run...
          Satan!

THUNDER cracks above them as Angels on
flying horses appear and celestial trumpets
BLARE.

                    GALEN (CONT'D)
          You're going back to your
          damnation!

SATAN smiles back at Galen and tilts his
head fiendishly. His leathery wings snap
out from behind him, spreading to their
full span, talons at the tips. His barbed
tail whips about.

The wafts of dark energy clear, revealing
Satan's satyr legs and cloven hooves. The
horns on his head become apparent.

More BOOMING explosions occur as Demons
emerge from the ground and scattered
wreckage. Despite the firefights, the
scattered dead bodies stand back up on
unsteady feet and slowly join the fight
against Galen and his Cohorts.

                    SATAN
          This is my home now...

He smiles a toothsome grin, maintaining
his fiendish gaze.

The Angels and Demons engage in battles
surrounding this standoff. Bolts of light
and dark energy crisscross the air.
SCREAMS of the strangest sorts punctuate
these battles as figures are injured or
die.

A squadron of mounted Angels swoops in
an arc and are blasted by a company of
Demons.

Wind whips the entire battle.

> GALEN

Now!

The Cohorts fire energy from their staffs, creating an orb of blue CRACKLING fire that encases Satan. He SCREAMS in pain and disgust, ANGER.

> GALEN (CONT'D)
>
> AD INFEROS TE!

Satan pushes back against this shrinking orb with his black waves of energy.

More Angels appear and add their energy beams to this Blue Orb. The Blue energy seeps out of the blades of the lances backwards and slowly engulfs the Cohorts wielding them.

> COHORTS
>
> (in chorus)
>
> AD INFEROS TE! AD INFEROS
> TE! AD INFEROS TE!

Some hold their long lances in vaguely phallic ways, males and females, as their eyes roll back in their heads, energy coursing, and firing upon the orb (a Heavy Metal album art masterpiece...).

More Demons fight against the appearing Angels and the Cohorts. Some of the Cohorts - from the hundred total - fight back, defending their fellows. Some die in loud EXPLOSIONS and SCREAMS.

Undeterred, Galen steps forward, training the Blue streaking energy from his lance on the orb that's trapping Satan.

                    GALEN
          The power of the Almighty
          commands you BACK TO HELL!
          AD INFEROS TE!
                    (pause)
          NOW!

The Blue Orb contracts, squeezing into
Satan's body, compressing the wafts of
dark energy spewing from him. The more
compressed the orb becomes, the more of a
solid Blue mold it creates around him as
Satan SCREAMS in pain.

The Blue encases Satan, his outstretched
wings, horns, arms, legs, and barbed tail
as he SHRIEKS in pain.

And then he lets out a hearty belly LAUGH,
as if breaking character.

A bolt of black energy fires out of the
orb and destroys a Cohort on Galen's right,
KAROLYNA (30).

Another bolt takes out someone on his
left. More bolts fire out of the orb as
Satan LAUGHS more.

Doubt flits across Galen's expression. He
maintains his weapon pointed at the orb,
but it's starting to fall apart. He glances
at the Angels flying about, fighting the
Demonic forces, some of which are also
flying.

                    COHORTS
          AD INFEROS TE! AD INFEROS
          TE!

With a BOOM a new regiment of Angelic
forces emerge from the grey storm clouds.
In the vanguard is a glowing white figure
of a Man holding a flaming sword. The
Cohorts' chant is joined by booming,
echoing voices in the heavens.

                    GALEN
          MY LORD, HELP US! GIVE US
          YOUR DIVINE POWER!

Galen scrambles for a crucifix which he
holds up while maintaining his aim with
the lance.

                    GALEN (CONT'D)
          AD INFEROS TE!

Blasts of Angelic energy are added to the
Blue Orb, helping it regain its shape.

And then Satan, using both of his hands,
jams a wave of dark energy into the
ground. The force lifts the ground, a
huge mantle of earth that flaps in waves,
throwing all who are on it to the sides as
if clearing off a picnic blanket.

Satan's wings SNAP, almost in emphasis, as
he hovers midair.

He fires another shock wave of dark energy
that knocks Galen and his Cohorts to the
ground, some of them exploding in death.

The Blue Orb falters and then dissipates
completely.

Satan fires off more dark energy at all
assailing him.

Galen clambers to his feet and retrains
his weapon as one-by-one his Cohorts SNAP
and EXPLODE around him into nothingness.

                    GALEN (CONT'D)
          No! You will NOT prevail--

Satan stares at him and fires a final
blast of dark demonic energy and Galen
EXPLODES, SCREAMING!

INT. THE MAELSTROM

Dark colors swirl in every direction.

Galen's failing SCREAM of anguish slowly dies off as he scrunches his eyes closed in defeat.

Pieces of him, a patchwork of him visible through a map of splotches and colors.

INT. HOSPITAL ROOM - DAY

A young black couple are expecting their first child. ALLIE (28) is resting in bed. TRAYVON (29) is holding her hand as she weeps. The news is on the TV and both are stricken with fear.

INT. THE VOID

Naked, collapsed on an endless white surface. Now it's ebony black. Now grey. Now red. It pops into different colors or blends gradually, constantly changing. Echoey choral VOICES sync with these changes.

Galen lies on the "floor." His eyes are open but unseeing, a crumpled dead man, on his side, slumped.

A woman's face appears to him.

SOFIA

...the rest of her body, her head, hair, is blurred away in the shifting void.

EXT. DRY LAKE BED - DAY

Sofia (30s) is dressed head to toe in a black suit, leaning down to address Galen, naked and slumped on the cracked and caked mud.

EXT. MILL POND - MORNING

Sofia is now in a flowing flower print gown, blown by the breeze, not just a dress.

Galen is slumped in the water. He SPLUTTERS and picks his head out of the water, catching his breath.

He scrambles, sits up, more COUGHING and SPLUTTERING. Glances about, wiping his mouth, face.

                    GALEN (CONT'D)
          Where am I? What happened?

Sofia just gazes on him placidly. After a moment...

                    SOFIA
          Nowhere. A lot.

INT. THE VOID - CONTINUOUS

Galen is sitting on the floor, his hands behind him, holding himself up, knees up, trying to cover his nakedness.

Sofia is still leaning down, addressing him. Now she's dressed in a linen peasant dress, her hair in a bun. Now she's in the black suit again. Now she's naked. Now she's in a green priestly robe.

Galen continues spluttering, more out of confusion, panic rather than aspirated water.

He's still wet. Now he's dry. He notices and blinks around at his surroundings.

INT. COZY DEN - EVENING

Now Galen is sitting in wooden chair. A

fireplace crackles. He's barefoot, in pants and a T-shirt. Sofia, across from him, a matching chair. The den, part of a stone and plaster house with wood beams defining the structure.

Galen, still disoriented but calmer in this "cozy" environment, looks around. Sofia's priestly robe is impressive.

                    SOFIA (CONT'D)
          Better?

                    GALEN
          What?

Sofia looks around, gesturing her meaning. Galen attempts to respond but thinks better of it. He focuses on Sofia. Her black suit is chic.

                    GALEN (CONT'D)
          Where is this? Where am I?

                    SOFIA
          Nowhere...yet.

Galen squints and then focuses even more on Sofia, peering at her more intensely.

                    GALEN
          Do I...

                    SOFIA
          ...know me?

Galen scowls, confused.

                    GALEN
          Yes.

She nods. Her suit is a dark grey now.

Galen's chair now has armrests that he grasps powerfully. He hangs on for dear life as he squints at Sofia and tries to

comprehend the situation. He juggles scores
of vital questions in his mind until
returning to one.

                    GALEN (CONT'D)
          Sofia?

She nods. Part of him softens, relaxes,
only to be replaced with more confused
tension.

                    GALEN (CONT'D)
          How...is this possible?
                    (pause)
          Where am I? Am I...

                    SOFIA
          Yes.

                    GALEN
          Dead.

She has a second thought.

                    SOFIA
          It's complicated.

She waits for him to comprehend. He
struggles with those other questions.

He FLASHES to Armageddon, Satan, his
Cohorts, the dying around him and that
final blast.

He jumps in his chair, startling himself.
He looks at her anew.

                    GALEN
          Was that real?

Shocking and disturbing him, Sofia purses
her lips, as if choosing her next words
carefully. She starts nodding.

                    SOFIA
          To you it was.

Galen glares at her comment. She smiles.

                    GALEN
          What was that?

Sofia inhales, calculating.

                    SOFIA
          Armageddon.
                    (pause)
          The final clash with the
          Devil.

Galen's eyes widen as she confirms his
memories.

                    SOFIA (CONT'D)
          You were tasked with
          recapturing Satan.

Galen gapes at her as his jaw slowly drops.
She nods.

                    SOFIA (CONT'D)
          After his escape, you and
          your...team were tasked with
          retrieving him, to return
          him to his home.

Galen frowns, searching.

                    GALEN
          But...I failed.

                    SOFIA
          What were you trying to
          do?

Galen thinks. He stares off...

                    GALEN
          What you said, I was
          trying to return him to
          his damnation, where he
          belongs.

                    SOFIA
          Why?

                    GALEN
          Because...he is the Cursed
          One. He was cast down... He
          is Beelze--

                    SOFIA
                (interrupting)
          Why are you doing that?

Galen gapes at her. She stares at him.

                    GALEN
          It's...my duty. It's my...
                (pause)
          ...atonement.

                    SOFIA
          For what?

FLASHBACK: Galen, a priest in 1400s Europe.
He's hung himself from a tree on a hillock
overlooking a meadow, his black cassock a
silhouette against green. End FLASHBACK

Guardedly, Galen looks at Sofia. She gives
nothing away. He chokes up.

                    GALEN
          My sins...

She just returns his gaze.

                    GALEN (CONT'D)
          My many sins...

He stares back at her. His grief and
contrition weigh heavily.

                    GALEN (CONT'D)
          I have to make up for what
          I've done.

                    SOFIA
          You failed.

He sobs and tries to choke it back. He
nods slowly.

                    GALEN
          I suppose I have.

He seems to give up.

                    SOFIA
          Is that it?

He stares off into space. He slowly hears
her and looks up.

                    GALEN
          What?

                    SOFIA
          Is that the end of your
          atonement? Are you done?

He thinks. He shrinks back.

                    GALEN
          No... I...

He searches for a better answer. He looks
up at her.

                    GALEN (CONT'D)
          What can I do? I failed.
          He...
                    (pause)
          ...destroyed me.

He thinks more clearly, but it's still so
confusing.

                    GALEN (CONT'D)
          He...killed me.

                    SOFIA
          So, you're dead.

She just watches him struggling.

He looks up.

> GALEN
> Yes... I suppose...

> SOFIA
> Then how are you speaking
> with me?

He attempts to respond but nothing comes out of his mouth. He frowns, at himself. He peers at the question in his mind.

> GALEN
> I'm not dead?

> SOFIA
> Are you?

Galen becomes distressed.

> GALEN
> I don't know! What is
> happening? One moment
> I'm...

FLASHBACK Galen's body is hanging from that tree.

He's in his armor standing, next to Karolyna, at a huge portcullis in what looks like Hell.

He's in mortal combat with the Dark Vortex.

He's blasted by Satan's dark energy. End FLASHBACK

> GALEN (CONT'D)
> And then I'm...

He looks around again and tests the validity of the armrests, his clothes, the room, the fire in the hearth, Sofia sitting across from him.

                    GALEN (CONT'D)
     ...here.

He gapes at Sofia.

                    GALEN (CONT'D)
     How is this possible?

               SOFIA
     All things are possible.

He frowns intensely, staring into space and
gradually arrives at a new thought.

               GALEN
     So, I can try again? I
     can...

He focuses on Sofia's gaze.

                    GALEN (CONT'D)
     ...go back and try to
     defeat him?

She nods at him casually.

               SOFIA
     Do you want to "go back
     and try to defeat him"?

               GALEN
     I do!

He sits up, committed.

                    GALEN (CONT'D)
     I must!

She nods.

               SOFIA
     You'll need help.

He gapes at her questioningly.

                    GALEN
                 (anguished)
          The Lord Almighty Himself
          and all of his leagues of
          angels were not enough to
          smother his evil.

                    SOFIA
          We need to go see some
          people.

He gapes again.

INT. THERAPIST'S OFFICE - DAY

JESSICA (35) sits in a comfortable chair
opposite TARA (40), her therapist.

Tears brim in Jessica's eyes. She blinks
them away.

                    JESSICA
          I avoid those gruesome
          photos in books. I've never
          seen that sort of thing.

She glances at Tara to confirm.

                    TARA
          How does this nightmare
          affect you?

                    JESSICA
          This...wasn't a nightmare.

Tara listens intently.

                    JESSICA (CONT'D)
          That was a memory. I saw
          the...burning.

                    TARA
          Do you believe in past-life
          regressions?

Jessica glances around, then at Tara.

                    JESSICA
          I didn't used to.

Tara nods.

                    JESSICA (CONT'D)
          Do you?

                    TARA
          That's not important.

                    (pause)
          But I do...

Jessica relaxes a bit.

                    TARA (CONT'D)
          How do you know you knew
          her?

Jessica blushes and smiles.

                    JESSICA
          I remember making love to
          her.

Tara is impressed and makes a note.

                    JESSICA (CONT'D)
          And then...I committed
          suicide.

Tara pauses, acknowledging that.

                    TARA
          How?

                    JESSICA
          Hanging.

Jessica thinks about that.

                    JESSICA (CONT'D)
          It was...the easiest way.

Tara nods and jots down another note.

                    TARA
          On what side was the noose,
          the knot?

Jessica thinks, and recalling, she
gestures.

                    JESSICA
          The left.

INT. EMERGENCY ROOM - DAY

ANGELICA (20s) is strapped to an
examination table. DR. JOHNSON (40) is
attending to her. Angelica is sedated and
calming down. Dr. Johnson holds her hand.
Angelica is freaked out but doing better.

                    DR. JOHNSON
          I want to monitor you as
          you come down.
                    (pause)
          It was just a bad trip.

She looks at Angelica with a compassionate
expression. Angelica nods uncertainly.

                    ANGELICA
          It felt so real.

Angelica FLASHES to hanging himself, as
Galen, in the 1400s.

Dr. Johnson nods pleasantly.

                    DR. JOHNSON
          It's a powerful drug.
                    (pause)
          You too much for your first
          time. But you're okay.

EXT. PENN STATION - DAY

WILSON (60) sits, slumped in his wheelchair
on the sidewalk, as New York City walks

by without noticing him. His old blazer is raggedy and his shoes are held together with old duct tape and plastic bags.

His eyes bounce from stranger to stranger, taking it all in and just as quickly letting go.

From behind, Sofia and Galen step up to Wilson and face him.

In no hurry, Wilson looks at them, not really caring.

Barefoot, GAP-outfitted Galen looks to black-suited Sofia as she smiles at Wilson.

                    SOFIA
          Take his hand...

She gestures to Wilson's closest hand and Galen steps closer, uncertainly.

                    WILSON
          Who are you?

Galen grasps Wilson's hand, which he instinctively raises and they look at each other.

The empty wheelchair sits on the sidewalk. Sofia, Galen, and Wilson are gone.

INT. EMERGENCY ROOM - CONTINUOUS

Dr. Johnson smiles at Angelica, patting her arm, consoling her as she steps away.

Sofia and Galen take her place. Angelica is alert, not anxious about them appearing there.

                    SOFIA
          Hi, Angelica.

                    ANGELICA
          Hi?

Sofia joins Galen's and Angelica's hands.
The examination table is instantly empty.

Dr. Johnson returns and immediately snaps
her fingers, trying to remember what she
was doing. She gives up; a "senior moment".

INT. THERAPIST'S OFFICE - CONTINUOUS

Jessica is standing, the end of her
session. Tara is getting up as Sofia and
Galen appear. Jessica turns, noticing them
and is surprised.

                    JESSICA
          What the f--

Tara too is surprised and then confused as
Jessica is no longer there.

                    TARA
          Same time...?

She does a double and triple take, actually
taking a few steps around her therapy
room.

                    TARA (CONT'D)
          Jessica...?

She moves to her desk and laptop and looks
at her calendar. That hour is empty which
makes her frown.

INT. THE VOID

Sofia and Galen are standing in this empty
space. Galen is checking himself, patting
his body. Sofia points and there's a
mirror. Galen notices it.

He steps closer. He's a biracial or

multiracial man with darker skin, than
before, but the same blue-green eyes.

He FLASHES back to the 1400s with Sofia
in an embrace. He's a German version of
his current new self, same cheekbones and
eyes.

Galen gazes at his face and gradually
accepts what he's seeing. He notices his
scar on his neck is now a birthmark. Sofia
is behind him and he glances at her.

                    GALEN
          What in creation...
                    (pause)
          Who are...were those people?
          Are they dead?

Sofia lets him figure things out.

He turns to her.

INT. DINER

Sofia opens the door and gestures for
Galen to enter. He looks at his bare feet
on the cold concrete.

She looks down, then at him. He looks at
her and then at his new shoes.

He's jumpy, looks around at the
establishment and the few people inside.
She gestures more emphatically and he steps
inside.

He glances at her uncertainly—

                    SOFIA
          Move.

He jumps and she leads the way, to a booth
at the far end.

He again looks to her for instructions. She

glares at him.

                    SOFIA (CONT'D)
          Sit.

She points to one side and she takes the
other with her back to the wall, facing
the street.

Galen fidgets, looks around warily. His
eyes catch her gaze. She stares.

                    SOFIA (CONT'D)
          Stop!

                    GALEN
          What?

He looks away...

                    SOFIA
          Look at me!

He looks. Then he focuses.

                    GALEN
          Where are we? What is this
          place--

She's neither annoyed nor casual, just
focused.

A WAITRESS steps up.

                    WAITRESS
          Hi, folks. Coffee?

Sofia turns, smiling.

                    SOFIA
          Two coffees and two
          breakfasts, eggs and hash
          browns. Sunny...

The Waitress approves of the succinct
order.

                    WAITRESS
          Coming up.

Sofia focuses again on Galen who is still
fidgeting like a bird. He focuses on her
again.

                    SOFIA
          Close your eyes.

                    GALEN
          Wha--

                    SOFIA
                 (interrupting)
          Focus! Close your eyes!

He tries to object but then relents.

                    SOFIA (CONT'D)
          Breathe!

                    GALEN
          Can I speak?

                    SOFIA
          No.
                 (pause)
          Ground yourself.

                    GALEN
          What?

                    SOFIA
          Focus and ground yourself.

                    GALEN
          Wha...what does that mean?

He starts to open his eyes. She snaps her
fingers at him.

                    SOFIA
          Close your eyes.
                 (pause)
          Do you remember praying?

                    GALEN
          Yes...ahum...

He nods, remembering that she told him not
to speak.

                    SOFIA
          That's the opposite of
          grounding yourself.
               (pause)
          You were trying to commune
          with God, your heavenly
          father, the heavens.

He grimaces, wanting to ask questions...

                    SOFIA (CONT'D)
          Imagine a silver chord of
          light from your loins to
          the center of the Earth.

His eyebrows peak and he relaxes, focused
on something specific.

                    SOFIA (CONT'D)
          There...

Galen breathes and calms himself.

The waitress returns, takes in the strange
goings on and leaves the two coffees.

Galen smells the coffee as his nostrils
flare.

                    SOFIA (CONT'D)
          You know what this place
          is.
               (pause)
          You now have four sets of
          memories to help you, but
          you already know this place
          as an eatery, a tavern if
          you must.

Galen's eyes dart about in REM. But he's

much calmer and nodding slightly.

                        SOFIA (CONT'D)
          Good.
                    (pause)
          You know...a lot, more than
          you did hours ago. More
          than you did centuries ago.
                    (pause)
          No! Keep breathing...

Galen was starting to fret but her
instructions calm him.

She waits... Minutes go by.

                        GALEN
          Those people...
                    (pause)
          Are me...

Sofia nods, impressed, she savors her
coffee, letting Galen simmer.

The Waitress returns with their plates.

                        WAITRESS
          Here ya go. Need anything
          else?

                        SOFIA
          No, thank you.

The Waitress smiles and leaves. Sofia turns
back to Galen.

                        SOFIA (CONT'D)
          Open your eyes.

Galen slowly opens his eyes, blinks and
looks down at the feast before him.

He's never seen something so scrumptious
and...clean. And yet, of course he has.

His hands go up reflexively and he's about

to grab the food.

                    SOFIA (CONT'D)
          Your silverware is right
          there.

Galen glances at her as if remembering,
stupidly. He spots the rollup.

                    GALEN
          Right...

He carefully unrolls the fork and knife
and acknowledges the napkin, as if
it's both completely new and totally
familiar. He looks around and spots the
napkin dispenser by the window and the
condiments.

He snatches the salt shaker and
contemplates it.

He looks at Sofia, sheepishly. Sets it
back.

Then the aroma brings him back and he
stops and inhales, eyes closed. He opens
his eyes and looks at her.

                    SOFIA
          Smell good?

                    GALEN
          Amazing...

He smiles. She does too.

He focuses on the coffee mug and picks
it up, again anew and familiar. He sort
of tries to hold it like a beer stein but
then thinks better of it. Body memory
competes for the best approach.

He holds it under his nose and inhales
deeply, eyes closed. This is different.

                    SOFIA
             Cream and sugar?

Galen's eyes pop open!

                    GALEN
          What?

Sofia points to ramekins of creamers and sweeteners. Galen studies them and then remembers, of course, what they are...

                    GALEN (CONT'D)
             No, thank you.

He focuses back on the coffee and with one last inhalation takes a tentative sip. It's hot but not too hot.

This time he closes his eyes purely out of delectation.

He looks at Sofia humbled and understanding. She smirks.

She nods at the eggs and hash browns as she digs into hers.

He thinks about the fork but then it all kicks in and he scarfs down the food.

They eat and sip quietly, mostly Sofia lets him, realizing that he can only manage so much stimulus at the moment.

He forgets his modern ways and reverts to the Middle Ages, stuffing his mouth, uncertain of when the next meal will be. But he also remembers to slow down.

He notices that Sofia knows this and shakes his head at himself.

                    GALEN (CONT'D)
             Delicious.

She nods.

                    GALEN (CONT'D)
          I don't know what to say
          about it...

Sofia listens.

                    GALEN (CONT'D)
          I've never tasted something
          so delicious.

He grimaces, remembering several moments.

                    GALEN (CONT'D)
          And yet, I have.

He's almost done and sops up the eggs
with his buttered toast, filling his mouth
again, like a peasant.

His eyes land on Sofia's plate. She
chuckles and shoves her remaining third to
him.

He glances at her, gratefully, and finishes
off her plate.

He stops and looks at her.

                    GALEN (CONT'D)
          Are you like this?

She gapes at him.

                    GALEN (CONT'D)
          The...memories? The...lives?

She nods and looks out the window at the
bustling city and planet...

                    SOFIA
          I...remember all of it.

Galen stops in mid scarfing... and gapes
back at her, astonished. He attempts a
question but stops. He looks at his own
thoughts and tries to understand rather
than burden her with his ignorance.

She turns to look at him.

                    GALEN
          What does that even mean?

She becomes casual about it. A chuckle.

                    SOFIA
          It means...a lot.

Galen tries to finish the last morsels when
a thought occurs to him.

                    GALEN
          You remember us?

She inhales and contemplates the full
breadth of his question and nods.

                    SOFIA
          Yes...

Galen sits back, thinking, needing the
support of the booth.

FLASHBACK: Sofia in her 1400s Spain form
burning to death at the stake thanks
to the Inquisitors. Galen hiding behind
a crowd, clearly seeing her and the
Inquisitors. End FLASHBACK

Galen looks like he might throw up. He
gulps and controls himself, thinking.

Sofia looks at him with a bemused
expression. He slowly meets her gaze.

                    GALEN
          Do...you remember...the end?

She nods.

He winces.

                    GALEN (CONT'D)
          Did you...

FLASHBACK: Galen gapes back at Sofia, distraught, through the heatwaves. End FLASHBACK

                    SOFIA
          See you? Yes.

He sobs. It's followed up by a more violent sob and tears. Behind the counter, the Waitress' head turns to him. He clutches his hands to his mouth.

                    GALEN
          Ohgodohgodohgod, no...

He forces himself to hold her gaze. His tears flow completely.

The Waitress comes by with more coffee and immediately about faces. Sofia notices.

She grabs some napkins from the dispenser. Presents them to him.

He grabs them and buries his face in them.

                    GALEN (CONT'D)
                 (muttering)
          I'm so sorry, I'm so sorry,
          I'm so sorry...

She just looks at him like some pitiful creature. He coughs and sobs as he exhausts this wave of grief and remorse. As he comes up for air and looks at Sofia she just looks at him, matter of fact.

                    SOFIA
          You would have died too, or
          worse.

He gapes at her, thinking, remembering.

                    GALEN
          I...

FLASHBACK: Galen, in his filthy cassock,

hanging from a tree. End FLASHBACK

                    SOFIA
          I know.

He glares, confused.

                    GALEN
          What?

She takes a casual sip of her coffee.
Then...

                    SOFIA
          Your mortal sin!

He gapes at her.

                    SOFIA (CONT'D)
          Your suicide...

                    GALEN
              (dumbfounded)
          How?

She smiles plainly.

                    SOFIA
          I...looked.

He's astonished. He thinks.

                    GALEN
          What...did you see?

                    SOFIA
          Enough.

He grimaces, wondering.

                    SOFIA (CONT'D)
          Hell? Yes.

He seems to collapse or hug himself. He
looks around, hunted. Haunted.

                    SOFIA (CONT'D)
          Breathe!

He looks at Sofia. Again she is matter of
fact.

MONTAGE, 1481 SEVILLE, SPAIN

FARM: GALEN (28) is a German priest. He's
putting on his black cassock and pulling
his boots on, emerging from a stable. A
hand reaches and yanks him back inside.

STABLE: SOFIA (26) yanks him back to her
lips.

                    SOFIA (CONT'D)
          Love them and leave them,
          priest?

He pulls back and smirks at her.

                    GALEN
          Leave? You? Never...
               (pause)
          But duty calls.

She's holding her dress in front of her
nudity, mostly letting their bodies hold it
up as they stand at the stable's doors. He
glances down at her skin, taking the sight
in. He kisses her passionately again.

SEVILLE: The Inquisition enforcers of the
Holy Office, one on each side, man-handle
Sofia down the street through a CLAMORING
crowd of onlookers.

Distressed, Galen watches Sofia escorted,
bruised, unkempt, hands tied.

Anguished, he wants to say something but
stops short. He shoves his way through the
crowd.

PLAZA: Sofia has been tied to a post in
a pyre. She's in great distress from the

heat, smoke, and flames. The surrounding crowd JEERS and CURSES. The Inquisitors stand by, passing judgment.

Galen is crying, hiding on the outskirts of the assembled crowd. He's watching his lover dying.

She looks up as a last gesture and looks right at him through the heatwaves, oddly enough, with an expression of love.

That devastates him and he runs off.

FARMLAND: Galen stumbles across a meadow.

HILLOCK: Galen slips from a sturdy oak tree branch and his body jerks at the end of the rope he's tied around his neck.

THE VOID: Galen is dragged to a netherworld.

CAVE: Galen crash lands on dirt, a muddy floor. He slowly comes to and sits up. Its light sources are red and dim.

CAVERN: Galen gazes out over a gargantuan space, the world virtually vaulted by a stone ceiling. Far and near WAILS and CRIES fill the air, pools and pits of fire and brimstone dot the terrain.

A hot fetid wind whips Galen's hair on his sweaty face.

PORTCULLIS: Galen is now fully encased in his Hell armor, a flowing organic pattern of corpuscular fibers all over his body. His helmet most closely resembles that of the Greeks, nose and cheek guards reaching down to his jawline.

He's standing with a partner, Karolyna, at a huge portcullis. Behind it, inside this cell, sits the Dark Lord on a throne, but captive.

Scores of other guards stand at attention.

This portcullis and cell are the summit of a mountain, a ziggurat, a stalagmite at the center of Hell.

End MONTAGE

Galen is distraught.

                    GALEN (CONT'D)
          How is that possible?

                    SOFIA
          How is what possible?

                    GALEN
               (exasperated)
          How can you know? How
          could you see?

He holds his head in his hands, gazing at her. A bystander would think he's horribly hungover and she's chiding him.

Plainly...

                    SOFIA
          All things are possible.

He winces, as if poked or shocked. Splutters.

                    GALEN
          Poss-- You saw me...there?

She hems and haws her head, considering.

                    SOFIA
          Think of an elephant.

Galen blinks, confused. He shakes his head and faces her.

                    GALEN
          What?!?

                    SOFIA
          It's like that.

                    GALEN
          Like what?!?

                    SOFIA
          Think of an elephant!
                    (pause)
          Do you see one in your
          mind?

He stops, cools his jets.

FLASHBACK: Galen from the 1400s, in a field
somewhere, can't imagine an elephant. He's
never seen one.

Wilson in his wheelchair can.

So can Angelica and Jessica. End FLASHBACK

                    GALEN
          Yes...?

                    SOFIA
          It's kind of like that.

He frowns, less and more confused.

She sits back, contemplating, comfortable.

                    SOFIA (CONT'D)
          Once I crossed over it was
          all clear and pure and
          joyful...again.

Galen listens.

                    SOFIA (CONT'D)
          I was...home, so to speak.

Galen is struggling to understand.

                    SOFIA (CONT'D)
          Stop thinking!
                    (pause)
          REMEMBER.

He gapes at her, but that does make a
difference.

                    SOFIA (CONT'D)
          In that state, asking what
          happened to you was simple
          and easy. Sort of like
          watching a movie.

She holds her coffee mug up to the
Waitress and gets a nod.

The Waitress arrives, pours Sofia's coffee
and...

                    WAITRESS
                (to Galen)
          Coffee?

He snaps out of it and composes himself in
his 1400s manner.

                    GALEN
          Yes, please. Thank you.

He holds up the mug as Sofia did and the
Waitress expertly and maybe with a little
flair pours a new piping hot cup to the
brim. Galen is fascinated by it all.

With a smile the Waitress turns and leaves.

                    GALEN (CONT'D)
          How much...

Galen frowns remembering what he's asking
about. Sofia savors her sip of coffee.

                    GALEN (CONT'D)
          How much of my...damnation
          do you know of?

She thinks and chuckles.

                    SOFIA
          "Damnation!"

                    GALEN
               (angry)
          Why do you scoff?

She looks into his eyes without any
hostility or charge.

                    SOFIA
          I know as much as I care
          to know,...or not.

He doesn't understand.

                    SOFIA (CONT'D)
          You went there...because you
          believed in it.

She drops that in his lap and waits. He
chews on it.

                    SOFIA (CONT'D)
          Your damnation... A
          period of suffering and
          recrimination and guilt and
          shame.

Her eyes widen dramatically, the diner
seems to darken as the light fixture
overhead brightens, despite the daytime.

He notices.

                    SOFIA (CONT'D)
          Your promotion to guard was
          nothing of the sort. He
          punished you, and your ilk,
          further not because it was
          a sin but because of your
          inaction.
                    (MORE)

                    SOFIA (CONT'D)
          The Vatican claimed that
          suicide is a sin because
          taking your life is not
          yours to do.
                    (pause)
          On the other hand, no one
          likes fence sitters, the
          noncommittal. He definitely
          doesn't like them. He's all
          or nothing.

She smiles at Galen's discomfort.

                    SOFIA (CONT'D)
          If you believe in Him.

Galen scowls, confused.

                    GALEN
          I was there!

                    SOFIA
          Of course! You believe
          that.

He ponders and settles with his hot coffee
mug in both hands on the table, staring
into the dark swirly liquid. Actual steam
rises from the mug. It's hot and he
releases the mug to only grip it again,
testing his limits.

Sofia lets him as she enjoys the moment,
her coffee, and his discomfort.

                    GALEN
          The fiery pits of hell...

Sofia smiles furtively. She hides the smile
as Galen looks up at her.

                    GALEN (CONT'D)
          You must think me the
          fool...

She looks at him pleasantly and then shakes her head.

                    SOFIA
          Belief is far more complex
          than foolishness.

Galen seems exhausted from the emotional roller coaster he just rode. But he's questioning.

She holds up two fingers.

                    SOFIA (CONT'D)
          I can try to persuade you
          off of a belief.
               (pause)
          Or you can remember...

She drops her hand. Galen blinks at her.

                    SOFIA (CONT'D)
          If I say that wasn't real,
          you'll never believe me.

He listens.

                    SOFIA (CONT'D)
          You lived it.

Galen is about to accept that as a confirmation, but stops short. He gets clever...

He looks at Sofia.

                    GALEN
          I believe I lived it.

She nods calmly.

                    SOFIA
          The same way that you
          believed that you had
          condemned yourself to
          damnation.

She lets that land on Galen. She finds
refuge in her coffee mug, holding it with
both hands close to her nose, savoring it.

He lets it land on him as well.

                    SOFIA (CONT'D)
          Is your soul eternal?
          Immortal?

Galen is caught off guard. He blinks as he
considers that.

                    GALEN
          Yes?

                    SOFIA
          Then what does it matter
          that you killed yourself?

She sips and gazes at him over her
steaming mug. He gazes back at her.

He looks away. He FLASHES back to his body
hanging from the tree.

He snaps out of it, looking up.

                    GALEN
          Now what?

She cocks her head.

                    SOFIA
          Apparently, He's out here
          now.

She looks at the TV monitor on the wall:
CNN's WOLF BLITZER with an "Armageddon"
graphic and chyron. The TV has UNMUTED
somehow.

                    WOLF BLITZER
          The war of all wars rages.

Three representatives, a RABBI, a PRIEST,
and an IMAM are on the panel with Blitzer.

Galen's hand searches for his crucifix.
It's not there.

                    PRIEST
          By all accounts...this is
          Judgment Day.

The Waitress pauses and gazes at the TV,
confused. Galen makes note of the priest,
an archbishop.

                    WOLF BLITZER
          There are reports of other
          conflagrations around the
          world, hot spots that have
          erupted without warning.

Each religious representative does some
form of prayer or genuflection in response
to such news.

                    GALEN
          And I have to stop Him.

She almost smiles in agreement.

                    GALEN (CONT'D)
          How?

Sofia's eyebrows arch excitedly.

                    SOFIA
          Why are you not in Hell
          right now?

Galen attempts to answer enthusiastically
and realizes he wasn't expecting that from
her.

He frowns, surprised and confused. She just
gazes at him patiently.

                    GALEN
          I...

                    SOFIA
          Failed.
                    (pause)
          You haven't atoned.

Galen sits back, troubled, thinking,
pondering.

                    GALEN
          I should be back down
          there...

He looks at Sofia who is giving him
nothing by way of an expression or
emotion.

                    GALEN (CONT'D)
          If I'm not there and...
                    (pause)
          I'm not dead...
                    (pause)
          ...and I failed to atone.

He frowns as he arrives at some
conclusions.

                    GALEN (CONT'D)
          Are you saying that it's
          not...

                    SOFIA
          I'm not saying anything.

He looks at her, checking her.

                    GALEN
          No, you're not.

                    (pause)
          Something else is afoot.

                    SOFIA
          That tracks.

                    GALEN
          I was damned to hell.
                    (pause)
          I was sent to capture the
          Evil One. And return him
          to his captivity. We all
          were.
                    (pause)
          And failed to do that.

Sofia nods slowly.

                    SOFIA
          How does Satan escape from
          Hell?

Galen launches into a reply but stops
himself.

He stares at his hands for a long time.

                    GALEN
          It's a charade...

Sofia smiles slightly.

                    SOFIA
          Come again?

He looks up at her and collects his
thoughts and emotions.

                    GALEN
          It's not real.
                    (pause)
          It's an act.

The Waitress, disturbed, MUTES the TV
again. Sofia gestures to it.

                    SOFIA
          It seems pretty real.

Galen gazes at the TV.

FLASHBACK: Galen in the 1400s is leafing through an illuminated text in a church.

A young and healthy Wilson is watching an old Motorola TV set behind a bar.

Jessica is sitting in a movie theater.

Angelica is editing a video. End FLASHBACK

                    GALEN
          It's staged, like a play.

Sofia smiles genuinely.

                    SOFIA
          When is a play over?

Galen thinks about that. He looks at her intently.

                    SOFIA (CONT'D)
          What gives a play its
          power?

Sofia sips her coffee as Galen's gaze shifts to the middle space, his thoughts grinding away.

He looks at his hands and articulates his fingers. He caresses his fingertips softly and then makes a tight fist.

                    GALEN
          What should I do?

He looks Sofia in the eye.

                    SOFIA
          You SHOULDn't do anything.

He cocks his head. She returns his gaze.

                    SOFIA (CONT'D)
          "Should" has gotten you
          this far.

He listens patiently; a new phenomenon.

                    SOFIA (CONT'D)
          You should have kept your
          vow of celibacy.
                    (pause)
          You should have saved the
          woman you loved.
                    (pause)
          You should have honored
          your life.
                    (pause)
          You should have guarded
          your charge.
                    (pause)
          You should have fulfilled
          your mission.

He contemplates each point she's making.

                    SOFIA (CONT'D)
          You should have succeeded.

He ponders all of that quietly, intently.
He's almost a stone statue, staring at his
life.

Sofia is casual and unconcerned. She smiles
at his struggle.

As if hearing or seeing something he
clears his throat.

                    GALEN
          I should have...married you.

He looks up at her. This is different.
Sofia sits up, sort of recognizing
something about the man in front of her.

He gulps. She smiles genuinely and nods.

                    SOFIA
          That's one option.

He slowly, carefully constructs his

thought.

                    GALEN
          That...was the only...truly
          happy...option.

FLASHBACK: In the 1400s an alternate
Galen is married to Sofia and they have
three children, living on their farm. End
FLASHBACK

She's caught a little off guard.

                    SOFIA
          Indeed. That...was...
                    (pause)
          ...a truly happy option.

Galen takes Sofia's hand in his and holds
it. He not so much caresses it as he
studies the realness of it and of her and
them.

                    WAITRESS (O.C.)
          Can I get you lovebirds
          anything else?

                    SOFIA (CONT'D)
          No, thank you.

Galen releases her hand but not the
feelings and thoughts. The Waitress drops
the old-timey bill, clears their plates and
leaves.

INT. HOTEL SUITE - EVENING

Galen and Sofia are enjoying an extended
session of lovemaking, something fueled by
centuries of longing and experiences.

They do the prerequisite kissing and
making out interspersed with the more
erotic throes of passion and physicality.

As Galen engages with Sofia he has flashes

of himself, the German priest with Sofia, the Spanish farmgirl, in stolen, clumsy forbidden moments.

He sees different versions of Sofia, different complexions, but always the same eyes. Some are different eras. Some are right in this same bed.

Now he's Angelica with Sofia.

Now Sofia is an African man with Jessica.

Now Wilson is with his late wife.

Now Galen is back with Sofia and they climax into an LSD-type funnel of dimensional realities.

...they sleep.

MONTAGE

Galen, just after Sofia's execution, clutches a rope, kneeling in prayer, in the meadow.

> GALEN
> Why, God? What is the point
> of this matter, Lord?

Jessica is crying, watching a horrible news report, video of children crying.

> JESSICA
> Oh, God. Why?

Angelica is wearing a goofy outfit at Burning Man. Sad.

A younger Wilson is standing at his wife's gravesite. Other mourners are stepping away, giving him space. Tears drop from his eyes.

> WILSON
> Why, Jesus? Why?

Galen is in a huge cave that is open to a hazy sky. Ancient steps, a ziggurat, stand before him. His clothing flickers, changing from moment to moment, representing his various lives and experiences.

He takes a big step, as if he could reach the first stage of the ziggurat and it shrinks or he grows. He takes another struggling step and reaches it, and the next, and next, and so on. The ziggurat is now a staircase that Galen easily ascends.

And now the treads and risers are shrinking as it widens and he keeps climbing into the bright light and away from the dark cave.

Images of Anguish and War assault him as he climbs. From the earliest civilizations worshiping different gods to the Catholic Crusades and the oceans of bloodletting from so many massacres to conflicts all over the planet.

Napoleonic battles and the grotesque aftermaths. WWI with the ghastly trenches and mustard gas attacks and deaths.

WWII: American soldiers using flame throwers on Japanese caves; the bombing of Dresden.

The Hiroshima mushroom cloud in black & white.

Modern battles, mostly carried out by US troops and weapons.

And the conflagration of Armageddon in Palestine.

Galen is horrified by all of it.

Then different images appear to him. A father holding his infant child. A mother playing with her son. Families laughing and crying from joy. People working together.

A nurse showing kindness to a patient.
A coach encouraging his athletes. People
rescuing an elk stuck in a wire fence and
cheering upon his release. An old campesino
flashing a gap-toothed smile. A variety of
lovers embracing and kissing.

Cells undergo mitosis. Suns explode.
Galaxies form. Mammals and sea creatures
frolic. A spermatozoa penetrates an ovum.

Galen is thrilled and enlivened by all of
that. He seems to stand taller, smiling,
tears of joy streaming down his face.

                    A VOICE
          People die...but life goes
          on.
                    (pause)
          The Lord gives and the
          Lord takes away...
                    (pause)
          That's the way He is.

Galen is brought up short, frowning.
Scowling. End MONTAGE

Galen stands at the dark suite's large
window, naked, looking out at the night
and the bright city. Despite the city
lights he can see the stars in the clear
night sky. His face is wet with tears.

                    GALEN
          It's so much...

Sofia gets out of bed, nude, and joins
him at the window. She embraces him from
behind, looking out at the world.

                    SOFIA
          You've been through a lot.

He takes her wrist in his hand and nuzzles

her. He kisses her arm and then faces her
and kisses her.

He holds her for a moment.

                    GALEN
          Why me?

She pulls away enough to look into his
eyes. His expression is one of genuine
humility.

She thinks for a moment.

                    SOFIA
          At that last moment...you
          asked for help.

Galen tries to remember.

                    SOFIA (CONT'D)
          Your soul, not your mind.
                    (pause)
          You asked...

She smiles at him.

                    SOFIA (CONT'D)
          ...and I heard you.

                    GALEN
          But... Why not Karolyna or
          any of my other cohorts?
          Or anyone else? Why me?
          They were just as...in the
          fight as I was...

She embraces him again.

                    SOFIA
          Sometimes things don't line
          up.
                    (pause)
          Sometimes they do.

                    GALEN
          Line up?

                    SOFIA
          You and I are connected.
          To something bigger.

                    GALEN
          But... Why? What am I
          supposed to do?

He steps away from her.

                    GALEN (CONT'D)
               (desperate)
          There's so much suffering
          and horror. And...there's so
          much love and joy.

Sofia shrugs.

                    SOFIA
          You're not supposed to do
          anything. It's up to you.

He sits on the window sill. She cradles
his head in her bosom. He savors embracing
her.

                    GALEN
          It's up to me.
               (pause)
          But...none of it matters.

She smiles.

                    SOFIA
          In a way. Yes.

                    GALEN
          Why do we do this? Come
          here?

She smiles again.

                    GALEN (CONT'D)
          ...to experience all of
          this?

                    SOFIA
          Correct.

He meant that as an unanswered question,
disbelief.

                    GALEN
          But, what's the point? So
          what?

                    SOFIA
          To learn. That's the point.

                    GALEN
          Learn what? And why?

                    SOFIA
          Have you not learned
          anything?

He contemplates that question.

                    GALEN
          Yes, but I'm not sure.

He stands up and disengages. He paces.

                    GALEN (CONT'D)
          You've helped me see the...
          artifice. The facade.

                    SOFIA
          Which "artifice?"

He stops and looks at her.

                    GALEN
          I used to believe in God,
          the Father, Son, and Holy
          Spirit.

                    SOFIA
          So there's no God.

She smiles, mischievously.

                    GALEN
          No.
                    (abruptly)
          It's not a "He."
                    (surprised)
          It's just so much, much,
          much bigger than that.

She nods.

                    GALEN (CONT'D)
          It's...all of this.

He gestures all around, the city, the
stars, them, the suite. He holds his hands
up again and studies them.

                    GALEN (CONT'D)
          It's what makes all of this
          possible.
                    (pause)
          But why the suffering? Why
          so much of it?

She breathes and then...

                    SOFIA
          That's the result of
          forgetting.

He stops and looks at her. He nods slowly.

                    GALEN
          We have forgotten that we
          made all of this.

                    SOFIA
          Correct. When you forget
          that, you take everything
          much more seriously. Too
          seriously.

                    GALEN
          Or...too real.

                    SOFIA
          Exactly.
                    (pause)
          But it's up to you.

He steps to the window again.

                    SOFIA (CONT'D)
          That's the one Law.

He looks at her.

                    SOFIA (CONT'D)
          Choice. Will. Free will.

He considers what she's saying.

                    SOFIA (CONT'D)
          Nothing is forced. Nothing
          is a should. Not in the
          larger realm.
                    (pause)
          Unless you agree to it for
          some reason, any reason.

He looks away, exasperated. Then he turns
back to her.

                    GALEN
          I agreed to go to Hell?

She nods, matter of fact. He stares at her
and slowly looks away.

                    GALEN (CONT'D)
          Why are you here...again?

He looks into her eyes.

                    GALEN (CONT'D)
          Why come back?

She chuckles.

                    SOFIA
          It's fun.

She steps up to him, embraces and kisses
him.

                    SOFIA (CONT'D)
          It's very difficult to do
          this in spirit form.

                    GALEN
              (offended)
          That's it? The physicality?

She laughs.

                    SOFIA
          "That's it?"
              (pause)
          That's HUGE!

She gestures to the entire universe as he
just did.

                    SOFIA (CONT'D)
          You said it! "It's so much!"
              (to herself)
          You have no idea...

He considers her point and then,
surprisingly, chuckles.

                    GALEN
          I guess so.

She gives him a long lingering kiss which
he returns completely.

                    SOFIA
          See?

                    GALEN
          I do.

                    SOFIA
          And yet...

He slumps, frowning slightly.

                    GALEN
          Yes.

EXT. NEW YORK CITY STREETS - NIGHT

Galen is dressed, wearing a coat and scarf, walking down the nighttime sidewalk. People are hurrying about.

MONTAGE, Galen is in Munich, across the street a family is standing at a bus stop.

Santiago, a family is standing at a bus stop.

Istanbul, a family is standing at a bus stop.

N'Djamena, a family is standing at a bus stop.

Isfahan, a family is standing at a bus stop.

Shanghai, a family is standing at a bus stop.

Galen is standing across the street from an empty bus stop.

HOSPITAL Allie and Trayvon are watching the news. The OBGYN is with them, holding Allie's hand. She reaches over to the remote and turns off the TV. Trayvon nods and Allie rests her head on his shoulder. End MONTAGE

                    HOMELESS GUY
          God doesn't exist!

Galen turns to see a HOMELESS GUY (30) sitting against a building.

                    GALEN
          How so?

                    HOMELESS GUY
          Why would God create us to
          piss and poop?

Galen is surprised. The Homeless Guy gapes
at him, mischievously.

                    HOMELESS GUY (CONT'D)
          That's some Charles Darwin-
          type shit.

He winks at Galen. Galen smiles uncertainly
and turns away.

In the store windows TVs broadcast the
latest news of Armageddon still raging. He
crosses the street for a better look.

In front of the plate glass he stares at
the muted images, both satellite and high-
altitude plane video. Galen frowns at this.

He's walking down another sidewalk, head
bowed. He looks up and realizes he's
standing in front of a Catholic church, a
cathedral. Its doors are open. He climbs
the steps and enters.

INT. CATHEDRAL

A night time mass is letting out. The
parishioners are CRYING and SNIFFLING.

Galen casually crosses the narthex and up
the nave and stops at the crossing. He
turns around and takes in the grandeur of
the structure.

FLASHBACK Galen young and in Germany in
the Cologne Cathedral under construction;
he's part of a visit by young priests. He's
looking around, taking in the grandeur of
the construction. End FLASHBACK

                    BISHOP (O.S.)
          Can I help you?

Amused by the word "help," Galen turns
and sees a BISHOP (50), in his cassock and
tunicle, smiling, welcoming.

The Bishop studies him closely, recognizing
a troubled soul.

                    BISHOP (CONT'D)
          We're in a glorious time,
          my son.

                    GALEN
          Are we?

The Bishop steps closer, questioningly.
Galen looks around.

                    GALEN (CONT'D)
          I thought "Armageddon" was
          a spiritual battle...
                    (to the Bishop)
          ...not a literal war...

The Bishop's eyebrows peak and he gestures
with both hands.

                    BISHOP
          The Divine Plan is unfold--

                    GALEN
                    (interrupting)
          "People die...but life goes
          on.
                    (pause)
          "The Lord gives and the
          Lord takes away...
                    (pause)
          "That's the way He is..."

The Bishop frowns slightly.

                    GALEN (CONT'D)
          ...Excellency.

The Bishop adjusts his attitude, maybe Galen is a priest.

                    BISHOP
          Are you questioning your
          faith, my son?

Galen chuckles, almost fully laughing, shocking the Bishop who frowns back at him.

Galen starts to leave.

                    GALEN
          Thank you, Bishop.

EXT. SKYSCRAPER ROOFTOP

It's a lookout area. Galen leans on the parapet, contemplating the city lights.

Sofia steps up to him, dressed in a gorgeous coat, scarf. He turns to her.

                    GALEN (CONT'D)
          You found me.

She smiles.

                    GALEN (CONT'D)
          How can I travel...the way
          I have?

She cocks her head.

                    SOFIA
          You're still technically...
          "in-between." You haven't
          come back yet.

He frowns slightly.

                    GALEN
          That your doing?

                    SOFIA
          No.

She looks into his face.

                    SOFIA (CONT'D)
          You haven't made that decision
          yet.

He frowns more.

                    GALEN
          To...

                    SOFIA
          Come back. Be here...again.

He thinks. He turns back to the city.

                    GALEN
          "Armageddon" is still
          raging...

                    SOFIA
          Apparently it's spreading.

He squints and looks at her. She returns
the look.

                    GALEN
          I...feel that I have to
          do something. I was this
          close...

He clutches a fist in the air. She nods.

                    SOFIA
          What do you "have" to do?

Galen looks around, searching, unsettled,
frustrated.

                    GALEN
          I...can't just let it go.

She studies him.

                    SOFIA
          You don't want to.

He checks in with her, enlightened.

                    GALEN
          I suppose so.

He thinks hard. He winces at the
memories...

                    GALEN (CONT'D)
          After...being sent to Hell
          and then tasked with
          recapturing...Him, and
          failing.

...but they don't affect him in quite the
same way anymore. He looks at Sofia.

                    GALEN (CONT'D)
          I know it's not what I
          thought it was. But I don't
          know what it is. And I
          need to find out.

                    SOFIA
          "What it is"?

He leans in.

                    GALEN
          If all of this...is make
          believe. Or if all of this
          is "in-between."
                    (intensely)
          I know I'm talking to you,
          right now. Or at least, I
          think I'm talking to you...

                    SOFIA
                    (smiling)
          More than talking...

                    GALEN
                 (blushing)
        Yes.
                 (serious)
        This...is too much...to just
        step away, to move on.

She nods agreeably.

                    GALEN (CONT'D)
        I need to find out what
        more there is. Why?

                    SOFIA
        How will you do that?

Galen thinks and straightens up, arriving
at a conclusion.

                    GALEN
        I have to go back and--

EXT. PALESTINE - CONTINUOUS

Galen is back in his blood-spattered hell
armor wielding his lance in the middle of
Armageddon.

Satan is aloft, throwing bolts of dark
energy at various assailants, humans and
angels alike. He even takes out some
demons, for the hell of it.

Galen looks up and for some way to reach
that height, but there's nothing.

He looks at Satan, shielding his eyes from
the blasts of energy filling the war-torn
sky.

                    GALEN
                 (hollering)
        HEY!
                 (pause)
        Hey, YOU!

Galen points with his lance. In the sky
Satan whirls and looks around.

                    GALEN (CONT'D)
          Yes! You!

Satan glances down. Spotting Galen, he
frowns and cocks his horned head as his
smile falters. He squints and drops to the
ground in front of Galen.

                    SATAN
          You?

Satan towers over Galen and paces around
him at leisure, every so often firing off
dark energy bolts without looking.

                    SATAN (CONT'D)
          I destroyed you...

Having said it Satan now rethinks that.

                    SATAN (CONT'D)
          How is it possible...?

Galen is intimidated by the entire fulsome
fearsome spectacle but tries to hold his
ground.

                    GALEN
          "All things are possible,"
          I'm told.

Satan scowls and seems impressed.

                    SATAN
          Indeed...

He looks Galen over, his armor, and the
lance he's wielding. He leans in, sneering,
and gestures theatrically with his taloned
hands.

                    SATAN (CONT'D)
          And what exactly is

possible now?

Galen reconsiders. He steps back and tentatively points the lance at Satan, knowing full well it wasn't enough before... Satan giggles like a kid.

                    SATAN (CONT'D)
          Komm jetzt, Priesterjunge!

Satan waves his fingers "come hither" and sticks his tongue out at Galen as he steps closer.

The huge figure of Satan, wings and tail, does the kindness of crouching down to meet Galen's height as he points his lance. The conflagration of Armageddon rages around them.

Galen's eyes dart around desperately, looking for an option.

He points the lance to the ground surprising Satan who frowns, confused.

Galen fires a stream of that blue energy into the ground between him and Satan. A hole sinks from the impact site.

Satan is confused. He looks at Galen questioningly.

                    SATAN (CONT'D)
          What the fuck?

Galen steps forward and jumps in, disappearing, actually startling Satan who jumps back and cowers.

                    SATAN (CONT'D)
          Wait... What are you doing?

As if regaining his composure and authority, Satan gazes about his Armageddon maelstrom and fires off sporadic bolts of dark energy, stirring up the chaos.

INT. HELL

Galen lands on the same kind of dirt, muddy floor as when he first arrived in Hell, immediately wheeling around, lance ready, looking for Satan or any other threats.

He's standing in a wide open area of Hell with the center hill in the distance backlit by an unearthly glow.

Galen grimaces as the oppressive hot fetid wind blows. But there's no lamentations of souls, no suffering. The fire and brimstone seems like no one's stoked it.

INT. OBSIDIAN DINING HALL

Hell has collapsed into a single room made of polished black stone walls, floor, and ceiling. The lighting is indirect from gaps in the walls, ceiling, and floor.

Galen looks around wielding his lance. As he turns back there now is a long red stone dining table, for lack of a better word.

At the end is a chair that turns around dramatically. THE EMPEROR (65) is seated and looks at Galen.

Galen reconsiders the lance and places it on the red table.

The Emperor is dressed like a Roman Emperor, purple toga picta, tunica palmata, rings on his fingers, a gold laurel wreath corona radiata on his head.

He is an Italian, soulful eyes, dark brown greying hair and still in good shape.

He's slouched in the chair, a hand to his lips, thinking. Staring at Galen.

Galen stares back. He darts a look around again, just to make sure. He looks back at the Emperor.

                    THE EMPEROR
            How did you do that?

Galen remains silent. His eyes dart about while facing this man. He's still trying to reconcile the horrors he just left with this strange new development.

The Emperor leans forward, resting his chin in his palm, still studying Galen.

Galen takes a tentative step to one side, changing his perspective on the man. The Emperor's eyes never leave him. He moves to the other side and takes a chance to look at the gaps in the walls letting light in.

He looks back at the man and takes a tentative step closer.

Then another.

He reaches the halfway point of the table.

The Emperor shifts and joins both hands at his chin still looking right at Galen. He doesn't seem afraid in the least, just intensely curious and a bit surprised.

Galen is slowly accepting what he's looking at, a man sitting in a chair in a strange room. Galen suddenly looks around realizing: there are no doors.

Galen looks back at the Emperor who smiles ever so slightly.

                    THE EMPEROR
                    (in German)
            Galen Brand...
                    (pause)
            ...aus Germania...

Galen stops short. He furrows his brow and considers speaking.

Now the man is a Neanderthal Woman, now an African farmer, now a MesoAmerican girl, now a Sumerian King, now a Nordic warrior, now a New York businessman in a suit, and then the Emperor again.

                        THE EMPEROR
          And who am I?

                        GALEN
          Not Satan...

The Emperor chuckles.

                        THE EMPEROR
          No...

Galen continues walking and takes his time to circumnavigate around the Emperor's seat and stops on the other side of the table. The Emperor picks up staring at Galen as he comes around.

                        THE EMPEROR (CONT'D)
               How did you accomplish
               that?

Galen remains quiet, scowling, trying to figure out the situation.

                        THE EMPEROR (CONT'D)
               How does a pissant
               philandering German priest
               who takes his own life, is
               damned to Hell, becomes a
               member of the Cohorts of
               Hell, fails to recapture
               Satan, and gets destroyed
               wind up here in my
               presence?

Galen looks around the room and then at the Emperor.

GALEN
There is no Satan...

The Emperor rocks back and smiles
curiously.

THE EMPEROR
Then who was that who
destroyed you?

Galen thinks...

GALEN
You.

The Emperor acts offended and stands up
casually. On his feet he whirls around
dramatically and holds his hands up.

THE EMPEROR
Do I look to you as a
sweaty twenty-foot tall
winged and horned satyr?

He holds his index fingers as horns on his
head, sneering.

GALEN
A costume.

The Emperor stops moving. He frowns and
cocks his head.

THE EMPEROR
Costume?

He paces a bit. He gestures to the surface,
the world, Armageddon.

THE EMPEROR
Are you claiming that all
of that was some sort of...
stage play?

Galen looks at the ring on the Emperor's
other hand, holding his toga. He notices
the Chi-Rho cross on the ring, plain to

see. Galen gulps and hides his reaction.

But the Emperor notices and casually hides
the ring.

                    THE EMPEROR
          You were there, dear boy.

Galen squints slightly.

                    GALEN
          And I failed.

The Emperor listens and nods.

                    THE EMPEROR
          True.

                    GALEN
          So why wasn't I cast back
          to Hell?

The Emperor ponders the answer to that
question and then reaches for Galen's lance
at the far end of the table. It slides,
noisily on the stone surface and hops into
the Emperor's hand.

Galen braces himself.

                    THE EMPEROR
          You are tiresome, priest.

He aims the lance and fires a bolt of blue
energy into Galen's center.

Galen flinches -- the bolt streaks through
and ricochets off the wall behind him -- a
punch to the gut...except it doesn't hurt.

He straightens up, clutching is uninjured
belly and chest. He looks at the Emperor
and remembers.

                    SOFIA (V.O.)
          You're still technically...
                    (MORE)

                    SOFIA (CONT'D)
          "in-between." You haven't
          come back yet.

The Emperor is shocked. He discards the
lance with a CLATTER and points at Galen.

                    THE EMPEROR
          You're dead!

Galen flinches but steadies himself and
looks at the Emperor.

                    GALEN
          Am I?

The Emperor scowls at him and catches on
to Galen's meaning.

                    THE EMPEROR
          Quite!
               (understanding)
          Not dead. You're between
          worlds.
               (annoyed)
          HOW?!?

                    GALEN
          I should be going--

EXT. CATHEDRAL - MORNING

Galen is back and standing outside of the
cathedral he visited earlier. He looks
around and then at the facade of the
cathedral...

...and then he sees the Chi-Rho Cross
symbol in the masonry and in the stained
glass windows, centered in a rosette.

In the stone he reads: "In Hoc Signo
Vinces."

Galen's jaw drops open and he drops to his
knees.

                    GALEN
          "In hoc signo vinces. In
          this sign conquer."

Galen stares at the stone symbol.

                    GALEN (CONT'D)
          Constantine...

He settles back on his hands, on the
sidewalk. Freaked out morning commuters
pass him, barely checking to see if he
needs help.

Strange celestial trumpets BLOW, filling
the sky.

Galen gets to his feet and rushes inside.

INT. BISHOP'S OFFICE

The door opens and Galen stands there.
The Bishop in his house cassock is a bit
surprised at this unplanned visit.

                    BISHOP
          Can I help you?
                    (pause)
          Oh, it's you.

                    GALEN
          Excellency.

Galen steps inside and supports himself on
the backrest of one of the facing chairs
in front of the Bishop's ample desk.

                    GALEN (CONT'D)
          Constantine the Great. What
          can you tell me?

The Bishop is surprised.

                    BISHOP
                    (stammering)
          A history lesson...

He stammers some more, then...

                    BISHOP (CONT'D)
          Have a seat.

Galen considers it and then quickly sits
down, on the edge of the seat, ready to
leave. The Bishop notices but continues.

                    BISHOP (CONT'D)
          What do you know about
          him?

Galen FLASHES to Jessica, Wilson, Angelica,
and his 1400s self for help.

                    GALEN
          He was the...last Roman
          Emperor and he converted
          to Christianity.
                    (pause)
          Some say he was genuine
          and some say he did it
          to unify his new empire,
          the Eastern Roman empire,
          Byzantium.

The Bishop nods in recognition. He squints
at Galen.

                    BISHOP
          Which do you think it was?
          Genuine or cynical?

Galen stops himself from responding,
instead...

                    GALEN
          How did he persuade the
          Empire towards the faith?

                    BISHOP
          Constantine the Great was
          a powerful Roman Emperor.
          However you look at his
                    (MORE)

                    BISHOP (CONT'D)
          victory at the Milvian
          Bridge, he benefitted
          greatly from it and
          consolidated his power.
                    (pause)
          It's not a small thing to
          create a new capital...
          Constantinople...

Galen is still waiting for an answer. The
Bishop waves a hand in the air and smiles.

                    BISHOP (CONT'D)
          If the Emperor adopts a
          favorite chewing gum, more
          people will too.

                    GALEN
                    (smiling)
          As simple as that?

The Bishop reconsiders.

                    BISHOP
          Nothing is simple. But,
          yes.

He stands up and paces, looking out his
leaded windows.

                    BISHOP (CONT'D)
          While the pagan religion
          of Rome was ubiquitous, I
          think that polytheism will
          always be vulnerable,...

He turns to Galen.

                    BISHOP (CONT'D)
          ...in a philosophical sense,
          to monotheism.

He holds his hands up, all ten fingers
extended and closes them to present one
index finger held up.

                    BISHOP (CONT'D)
          Try managing a pantheon as
          compared to ONE.

He gestures to the whole thing.

                    BISHOP (CONT'D)
          When the big guy simplifies
          things, people get in line
          and maybe they don't have
          to keep marking their
          calendars, sacrificing
          goats and chickens to Mars
          and Diana.

Galen smiles, appreciating the Bishop's
sense of humor.

                    GALEN
          And then...two thousand
          years of conversion,
          colonization, genocide,
          persecution, and
          enslavement.

The Bishop blanches and leans against his
windowsill. He frowns and thinks and then
nods.

                    BISHOP
          Sadly, yes.
                    (pause)
          We are stewards of a
          problematic history.

Galen holds his gaze and nods slowly.

                    GALEN
          Problematic...

Galen ponders some more.

                    GALEN (CONT'D)
          Do you think he was
          cynical or genuine?

The Bishop gives in a bit. He smiles
abashedly.

                    BISHOP
          I have to admit. I think
          it was a cynical ploy
          to unify power. He was
          baptized late in life;
          although that was common
          for the Church back then.
          But it was convenient for a
          Roman Emperor to hold off
          as long as he could.
                    (pause)
          If any of that stuff
          mattered to him.

                    GALEN
          Mattered?

                    BISHOP
          He was a Roman Emperor. He
          was a learned man. He had
          access to all of the wisdom
          of the entire world at that
          time, the orthodoxy and
          the esoterica.

Galen listens more closely.

                    BISHOP
          And all of the experts he
          could possibly want.

                    GALEN
          Eusebius.

                    BISHOP
          Exactly. One of many.

                    GALEN (CONT'D)
          And you think he did it
          cynically...

The Bishop genuflects, closing his eyes
momentarily.

                    BISHOP
          God works in mysterious
          ways.

Galen chuckles. The Bishop notices and lets
it slide. He shrugs.

                    GALEN
          Indeed.

                    BISHOP
          Why do you ask?

Galen gets up to leave. He pauses suddenly
exhausted by it all.

                    GALEN
          I think he's still at it.

The Bishop hears that and then digests
what Galen actually said and does a double-
take. He stares, quizzically at Galen.

Galen nods and steps out of his office.

EXT. NEW YORK CITY STREET

Galen approaches the same store windows
with TVs broadcasting the latest news about
Armageddon. The video is from a drone, one
of several, sent into the melee.

                    WOLF BLITZER
          Our team has managed to
          send drones into this
          raging battle. None of our
          people are in danger by
          doing this. However, our
          drones are equipped not
          only with video but audio
          as well.

Galen gapes at this.

                    WOLF BLITZER (CONT'D)
          This is live footage from...
          Armageddon, which as we've
          reported has been growing
          in the Negev.

This drone is approaching the center where
Galen most recently faced Satan. The video
shows a flying figure. As it nears it
becomes clearer, the classic Devil image.

                    WOLF BLITZER (CONT'D)
          It's hard to believe that
          we're seeing this, but
          seeing is believing. To
          our viewers we seem to be
          looking at what so many
          religions refer to as the
          Devil, Satan. It or he
          seems to be flying and
          battling other forces, from
          the sky and the ground.

Galen makes a determination.

EXT. PALESTINE - CONTINUOUS

Again Galen is in the middle of
Armageddon, on the ground. But this time
he's still dressed in his coat, scarf,
and modern attire, no more hell armor and
lance. The wind, dust, and smoke whips
about, causing him to squint and cower.

He looks up in the air and again sees
Satan, raging against the various forces.

                    GALEN
              (hollering)
          Hello!

Satan is busy and there's a lot of NOISE.

                    GALEN (CONT'D)
          I said, HELLO!

Satan hears him and looks down again. Annoyed, he drops to the ground.

                    SATAN
          What do you want?!?

The news drones come in closer, documenting these developments. Galen notices them, particularly the closest.

Galen is having a hard time staying on his feet with all of the turbulence and nearby explosions, but he does his best.

He stares at Satan and smiles. Satan glowers back at him.

                    SATAN
          What do you want?

Galen smiles broader. The news drones capture various angles of this meeting. The closest one gets a great, clear close-up of Galen smiling at Satan.

INSERT: The news channel broadcasts this face-off between what looks like "The Devil" and a regular man in a coat being buffeted by the wind.

                    WOLF BLITZER
               We don't know who this
               intrepid man is. We're
               consulting with our experts
               on who this could be. If
               this really is Satan, who
               could be formidable enough
               to face him, to confront
               him so...fearlessly?

Galen takes a step forward. Satan again stands on the ground, but this time he doesn't crouch closer to Galen. He simply paces in front of him in his full height. He even SNAPS his wings to their full span.

                    SATAN
          What do you want? I'm busy.

Galen glances at the news drone and then
looks at Satan.

                    GALEN
          There is no Satan!

Satan smiles uncertainly. He whirls around
cockily, showing off his fantastic costume.

                    SATAN
          NO SATAN?!?

He whirls and ROARS at Galen in a
terrifying display of demonic evil.

Galen plants his feet apart and holds his
hands behind his back, at ease, smiling
placidly, unafraid. His only disturbance is
the grit and sand in the air, threatening
to get in his eyes, but that's it.

He still smiles at Satan.

                    GALEN
          There is no Satan!

Galen gestures dramatically with one hand,
finger pointed.

                    GALEN (CONT'D)
          You are NOT Satan! This is
          all an act!

Satan is enraged at Galen's insolence.

                    GALEN (CONT'D)
                (calmly)
          Go ahead.

Satan dramatically raises his right fist,
rears back, and then launches a bolt of
dark energy right into Galen.

The dense dark bolt of evil energy flies

right through Galen, hitting the dirt behind him. Satan sustains this stream of evil energy.

Galen just stands there smiling back at Satan.

INSERT: The News Broadcast is showing this sudden face-off.

Galen continues to stand there completely unaffected by the Devil's worst attack possible.

                    GALEN (CONT'D)
          You are a fake! A con! A
          scam!

INT. CATHEDRAL CAFETERIA/MEETING ROOM

The Bishop joins others gazing at a TV with the news on. His jaw drops.

EXT. PALESTINE - CONTINUOUS

Galen holds both hands up and turns completely around and then faces Satan again, showing the complete lack of damage caused by the Devil's most intense attack.

As if bored, Galen crosses his arms akimbo and watches Satan and his antics.

Satan continues firing his stream of demonic Devil energy with zero effect. The longer he persists, the angrier he gets until he gets fed up with the abject embarrassment of being shown up publicly.

He ROARS in anger and whirls around as he stops firing.

                    SATAN
          FUUCK! Fine!

In a sequence of violent arm gestures
and whirling about, Satan seems to wipe
away and turn off various elements of
this raging war and then he pops out of
existence with a loud BANG and the rest of
the Battle of Armageddon disappears.

The shockwave of this nothingness batters
the remaining humans on the battlefield
and the news drones recording everything.

INSERT: The news shows this sudden change.
They cut to Wolf Blitzer who is pale and
dumbstruck.

                    WOLF BLITZER
          Uh, ladies and gentlemen...
          We have no idea what just
          happened.

INT. CAFETERIA - CONTINUOUS

The Bishop watches thunderstruck.

                    BISHOP
          What the hell...

                    WOLF BLITZER (O.S.)
                    (gulping)
          One moment as you saw,
          we were witnessing what
          religious experts from
          various faiths were forced
          to accept was Judgment Day
          finally come, Harmageddon
          of the Bible...
                    (pause)
          And it seems to have
          stopped, disappeared.

Blitzer looks off-screen to his producing
staff.

> WOLF BLITZER (CONT'D)
> We still have no
> identification for this man
> standing in the middle of
> the Negev desert, dressed
> for New York weather...

EXT. PALESTINE - CONTINUOUS

The closest drone flies closer to Galen.

> WOLF BLITZER (CONT'D)
> Excuse me, sir. Can you
> hear me?

Galen turns to look at the drone's camera
and composes himself as the winds of war
and Armageddon have now died down and he
no longer has to squint at the flying dust
and sand.

> WOLF BLITZER (CONT'D)
> Our news drones are
> equipped with speakers, so
> this man should be able to
> hear me.
> (pause)
> Sir, can you hear me? Who
> are you? What is your
> name?

Galen smiles at the camera.

> GALEN
> Yes, I can hear you.

> WOLF BLITZER
> Who are you?

Galen disappears.

The drone backs off for a wider shot. It
even does a double-take, left right. The
producers cut to another drone showing
the primary drone floating in front of an

empty patch of the Negeb desert.

Troops are milling about, their weapons hanging from straps or dropped entirely. Some are embracing each other, some are approaching their former enemies, unsure of what to do, but definitely no longer fighting.

Some CHEERING can be heard and CRIES and WHOOPS of relief.

INT. HOSPITAL ROOM

Allie and Trayvon are hugging joyfully.

EXT. NEW YORK CITY STREET

Galen is back. The people in the street have all stopped in their tracks, having learned or learning the news.

Some run up to the store windows with the TVs. Others study their phones.

INT. HOTEL SUITE

Galen appears in the suite and sees Sofia napping on the bed.

He sits next to her and rouses her with a hand on her shoulder.

She opens her eyes easily and smiles at him. He smiles at her in a confused and happy way.

                    SOFIA
          You did something.

                    GALEN
          I guess I did.
                    (pause)
          It's over.

                    SOFIA
          I know.

                    GALEN
          You do?

She shrugs.

                    SOFIA
          I was watching.

He takes his coat and scarf off. He notices
they're still dusty from the desert. He
kicks his shoes off and lies next to Sofia
on the bed.

                    GALEN
          Was that real? Did that
          really happen?

                    SOFIA
          What do you think?

She's still curled in the fetal position
while he's lying supine, staring at the
ceiling.

                    GALEN
          I don't know anymore.

                    SOFIA
          Pish-posh. Balderdash!

He side-eyes her.

                    GALEN
          It was real.

She props herself up and smiles
victoriously.

Thoughts race through his mind and she
just lets him have them.

She places her hand on one of his, on his
chest. He looks at their hands and then
back at her.

                    GALEN (CONT'D)
          This is so...weird.

                    SOFIA
          What is?

                    GALEN
          ...reality.

She chuckles and nods.

                    SOFIA
          You have no idea...

She smiles almost mischievously.

EXT. STREET - EVENING

Sofia and Galen are walking along, quietly
witnessing the rest of the population going
about their lives. It's a strange sort of
daydream, intimate and not so intimate
details of everyday life. Genius moments
and foibles.

EXT. CAFE

Sofia and Galen are seated by a WAITER (40)
at a table separated from the sidewalk by
a half wall of planters. He leaves them
with their menus.

Galen is distracted by the people. Sofia
makes her choices and looks at him over
the menu. As usual, she gives him time,
his space.

He collapses, clutching his face in his
hangs, kneading his face with his fingers,
exhausted. His hands drop and he breathes.
He looks up and catches her studying him.

                    GALEN
          What?

He can only see her eyes over her menu.

She drops the menu, revealing a slight
knowing smile and shakes her head.

                    SOFIA
          You've been through a lot.

He looks away and nods.

                    GALEN
          I...used to believe.

He looks around at the various lives going
about.

                    GALEN (CONT'D)
          That we were...halved.
          Part of us clinging to
          the Divine. But the other
          part,...lost and corrupted.
          Unworthy.

                    SOFIA
          And now?

He turns to her and thinks.

                    GALEN
          We're...on our own. But,
          we're whole.

She purses her lips, considering his
answer.

                    GALEN (CONT'D)
          There is no Satan.

She perks up.

                    SOFIA
          How so?

                    GALEN
          All of that, flim-flam!
          There never was.

                    SOFIA
          Never? Armageddon?

He focuses on her.

                    GALEN
          Yes. Armageddon.

                    SOFIA
          People were dying.

He stops, thinks back. A twinkle appears
in his eye.

                    GALEN
          Been there. Done that.

Sofia chuckles.

                    SOFIA
          So, it wasn't real.

Galen ponders that as well.

                    GALEN
          It was...both. Real and...a
          projection.

                    SOFIA
          Projection.

                    GALEN
          We. I...contributed to that
          realness.

He FLASHES back to his bloodied Hell
armor and violent clashes leading up to
confronting Satan.

He sees his body hanging from that tree.

                    GALEN (CONT'D)
          What are WE doing here?!?

                    SOFIA
          WE're eating.

She stares him down. With a smile.

> GALEN
>
> It was Constantine.

Sofia nods.

> GALEN (CONT'D)
> (aghast)
> He's been at it this whole time.

> SOFIA
>
> At what?

> GALEN
>
> He's...been manipulating... the world.

> SOFIA
>
> Manipulating. Why?

He shudders.

> GALEN
>
> I don't know. POWER. Control.

> SOFIA
>
> No.

He looks at her.

> SOFIA (CONT'D)
> Sure, at first he was all about power.
> (pause)
> It's not just that.

Galen sits up, listening.

> GALEN
>
> How do you know this?

She gapes at him.

                    SOFIA
          I've been paying attention!

He accepts that as much as he can.

                    SOFIA (CONT'D)
          Long ago he became addicted
          to this... Reality.

She waves at their surroundings.

                    SOFIA (CONT'D)
          He knows there's only love
          in the entire universe.

She taps their table.

                    SOFIA (CONT'D)
          Love.

She taps the planter separating them from
the sidewalk.

                    SOFIA (CONT'D)
          Love.

She smiles at a couple walking by and
gestures to them.

                    SOFIA (CONT'D)
          Love.

Galen scowls.

                    GALEN
          How... But...the suffering.
          I saw thousands of years
          of...brutal carnage.

He looks at her in punctuation. She looks
back at him.

                    SOFIA
          He learned that Love is
          most...strident, most vivid,
          most real - in his
                    (MORE)

                    SOFIA (CONT'D)
          experience - when the world
          around it is the most
          cruel.

                    GALEN
          But God...

Galen chokes on his own words. He composes
himself and considers what he was going to
say.

                    GALEN (CONT'D)
               (to himself)
          God doesn't exist...

Sofia studies him. He looks at her and
starts anew.

                    GALEN (CONT'D)
          The Universe...doesn't care.

Sofia smiles.

                    GALEN (CONT'D)
          Wait. He's...turned this
          entire thing into his own
          plaything? His own toy?

Sofia sits up and leans in, smiling.

                    SOFIA
          See. That's what I love
          about you. Dumb where it
          doesn't matter, smart where
          it does.

Galen balks and then deciphers that.

The Waiter shows up. They look up at him,
interrupted.

                    WAITER
          Can I take your ord--

He's clearly nervous. He glances at Sofia

but then focuses on Galen.

                    WAITER (CONT'D)
          Sorry. You're...the guy.
          You're him. The one...on the
          news.

He pulls out his cellphone, stammering,
holding up a freeze-frame from the news.

                    WAITER (CONT'D)
          You're him.

Tears are brimming in his eyes. He drops
to his knees and clutches his hands in
prayer.

                    WAITER (CONT'D)
                (desperate)
          Oh Father, hallowed be thy
          name!

He looks at Galen and reaches out to grasp
his hands. Stops himself.

                    WAITER (CONT'D)
          Sorry. Please. Oh my god.
          Oh my god.
                (pause)
          Are you Jesus? Is this the
          Second Coming?

The rest of the people in the cafe are
focused on Galen, similarly wondering or
fascinated by him, having noticed him
already. Galen and Sofia look around.

                    GALEN
          Please. Don't.

                    WAITER
          I...I'm... Tell me what to
          do. I'm your servant...My
          LORD!

The Waiter has found an idea to focus on.

                    WAITER (CONT'D)
          How can I be of service,
          Lord?

He decides to completely avert his eyes
and bow as low as he can. Galen and Sofia
check with each other. Sofia is still
casual and leaves it up to Galen.

                    GALEN
          Uh, hey. What's your name?

He reaches out and touches the Waiter's
shoulder. He flinches and reaches up,
clutching Galen's hand, lovingly and
terrified.

                    WAITER
          My Lord.

                    GALEN
          Please stand up.

The Waiter looks up cautiously.

                    GALEN (CONT'D)
          What is your name?

                    WAITER
          Stephen.

                    GALEN
          Just...just. Please. Stand
          up.

The Waiter begrudgingly stands up, humble.

                    WAITER
          I'm sorry.

                    GALEN
          You have nothing to be
          sorry about.

Sofia watches the scene curiously.

                    WAITER
          I...

                    GALEN
          Stephen.

                    WAITER
          Yes, Lord.

                    GALEN
          Can we just--

                    WOMAN (O.S.)
          Oh my god! It's Him!

Galen and Sofia look and see a WOMAN on
the other side of the planter pointing at
Galen. The sidewalk has since clustered
with onlookers, half of them with their
cellphones recording the moment. Murmurs
of "It's Him" bubble from the crowd.

Galen and Sofia look at each other. They're
surrounded.

They get up and make their way out of the
cafe. The Waiter follows them, uncertain of
what to do.

                    GALEN
          Sorry.

EXT. STREET

Galen and Sofia are hurrying down the
street, followed by a growing crowd. People
in front of them stop and turn, holding
their phones, learning from the internet of
the encounter.

                    GALEN
          What is going on?

Sofia reaches for his hand.

                    SOFIA
          Here!

They disappear.

The mob SHRIEKS.

INT. HOTEL SUITE

Galen and Sofia plop back into their room.
Sofia whirls.

                    SOFIA
          I guess it's room service.

Galen is in shock.

                    GALEN
          What was that?

                    SOFIA
          "What was that?"

He collapses and sits on the bed. Sofia
approaches him, smiling.

                    SOFIA (CONT'D)
          You saved the world from
          ARMAGEDDON!

She lets that sink in.

                    SOFIA (CONT'D)
          What did you expect?

Galen thinks, blinking. And idea occurs to
him as he holds up a hand.

                    GALEN
          But...you took us there.

Sofia smiles, caught.

                    SOFIA
          Yeah. I was curious...

She plops down in one of their chairs, head and arms hanging off the sides.

                    SOFIA (CONT'D)
          That was wild.
                    (pause)
          You're the Second Coming.
          They think you're Jesus.

                    GALEN
          Wait! No!

She lifts her head, looks at him.

                    GALEN (CONT'D)
          That can't be...

A TRUMPET BLARE sounds, vibrating their windows. Sofia stands, followed by Galen. They approach the windows and see red streaks in the sky, a carnadine aurora borealis.

The WAILING of SOULS follows. Then more TRUMPET BLARES.

Sofia and Galen look at each other.

Sofia turns on the news.

INSERT: Wolf Blitzer looks distraught.

                    WOLF BLITZER
          Despite the recent
          developments in the
          Middle East it seems that
          the prophesied day of
          Armageddon may not be gone
          as we first thought.
                    (pause)
          We have our panel of
          religious experts on again
          to help us understand
          what's going on.

The cast of the proverbial joke is sitting

at the news desk again.

                    WOLF BLITZER (CONT'D)
          What exactly are we seeing
          now?

                    PRIEST
          We seem to be seeing
          a wider, world-wide
          manifestation of the End
          Days.

                    IMAM
          I concur.

                    RABBI
          Yes.

                    WOLF BLITZER
          This is real?

The three only gulp and nod.

                    WOLF BLITZER (CONT'D)
          Good Lord...

The news segment cuts to video from
around the world of demons emerging along
with fire and brimstone, lava explosions
in the middle of cities, the capitals of
countries. People are seen running for
cover, SCREAMING.

Galen and Sofia look at each other.

                    SOFIA
          He wasn't going to give up
          that easy.

Galen stares at her.

EXT. ICELAND - DAY

Galen and Sofia are on a grass plain at
the foot of extinct volcanoes.

                    GALEN
          Wait! What are we doing
          here?

He whirls around, orienting himself.

Sofia finds a chair and sits down. Galen
gapes at her and the fact that there's a
chair handy.

She nods behind him. He turns and there's
a chair for him too. He looks at her
warily as he moves to sit down.

                    GALEN (CONT'D)
          What is...?

                    SOFIA
          I've called a friend.

MICHAEL appears before them, fifteen feet
tall with white wings spread out. The wings
fade away and he shrinks to a "normal"
size as he finds a chair and sits down.

                    MICHAEL
          Sofia.

                    SOFIA
          Michael.

Galen gapes at both of them.

                    MICHAEL
          Hello, Galen.

                    GALEN
          Who...?

                    MICHAEL
          You already know.

                    GALEN
          Why?

                         MICHAEL
              You revealed a long dark
              secret.

Galen gapes at him and stammers.

                         MICHAEL (CONT'D)
              You revealed who has been
              behind most of your...recent
              history.

                         GALEN
              ...a man.

                         MICHAEL
              Correct.

                         GALEN
              Constantine.

                         MICHAEL
              Yes.

Galen gapes some more. Michael considers
his next words.

                         MICHAEL (CONT'D)
              You're free to move on,
              Galen. You don't need to
              stay here, on this plane.
                    (pause)
              But you seem to be hanging
              on. That's up to you.

Galen thinks.

                         MICHAEL (CONT'D)
              In the greater scheme it
              doesn't matter.
                    (pause)
              But you're pointing out
              that it might.

                         GALEN
              That what might?

                    MICHAEL
          There are two rules, two
          laws to the Universe: Love
          and Choice.

Galen nods tentatively.

                    MICHAEL (CONT'D)
          Constantine is pushing the
          limits of the second law.

Galen tries to keep up.

                    MICHAEL (CONT'D)
          He's forced billions of
          souls to give up their
          sovereignty and follow a
          narrative that suits him.

                    GALEN
          Reality.

                    MICHAEL
          His version of reality.

                    GALEN
          What other version is
          there?

Michael almost laughs and looks at Sofia.
She smiles back.

                    MICHAEL
          Any version!

Galen recalls Sofia:

                    SOFIA (V.O.)
          "All things are possible."

                    GALEN
          Any version?

                    MICHAEL
          Yes.

                    GALEN
          So... "All of humanity
          lives without strife
          or suffering, hunger,
          deprivation..."

Michael nods casually. Galen stops.

                    GALEN (CONT'D)
          You nod...so casually.

Michael chuckles this time.

                    MICHAEL
          "All things are possible."
                    (pause)
          You simply have to choose--

                    GALEN
                    (interrupting)
          Then why is there so MUCH
          pain? So, MUCH SUFFERING?
          SO MUCH--

                    MICHAEL
                    (interrupting)
          Because you...chose it. You
          all agreed to it.

Galen is gobsmacked.

                    MICHAEL (CONT'D)
          When all you remember is
          this life, from birth to
          death, it's very difficult
          to be...free. To choose...
          something else.

Galen listens closely.

                    MICHAEL (CONT'D)
          You remember more now.
          Don't you?

Galen nods slowly but suspects he's missing
something.

                    GALEN
          Remember what?!?

Michael smiles and stares at Galen. Galen
shrinks a little.

                    MICHAEL
          This...

He gestures to the whole wide world.

                    MICHAEL (CONT'D)
          ...is yours. To do with as
          you will.

                    GALEN
          What about my atonement?

                    MICHAEL
          For your sins?

Galen gulps, ashamed. Michael smiles
sympathetically.

                    MICHAEL (CONT'D)
          There is no punishment.

Galen shakes his head.

                    GALEN
          Karma.

                    SOFIA
          Karma is not punishment.
          It's balance.

He glances at her and then at Michael.

                    MICHAEL
          It's all about flowing
          and, if necessary,
          learning lessons. But not
          retribution.

Galen considers that.

                    MICHAEL (CONT'D)
          What did you learn from
          your time with Sofia and
          your suicide?

Galen thinks. He glances at Sofia and then
looks at Michael.

                    GALEN
          I...was misaligned. My
          priorities were misplaced.
                    (pause)
          I abdicated my role, my
          part in this.

Michael nods, impressed.

                    GALEN (CONT'D)
          So, why did he get to...
          create such a heinous
          thing?

Michael shrugs slightly.

                    MICHAEL
          Free will.
                    (pause)
          The one thing protecting
          Free Will is a single voice
          saying,...

Michael smiles mischievously, doing his
best New York accent.

                    MICHAEL (CONT'D)
          "Wait a second..."
                    (pause)
          He convinced you of a very
          limited reality. And very,
          very few of you question
          it.

                    GALEN
          But the dying and
          suffering.

                    MICHAEL
          All over...

Michael snaps his fingers.

                    MICHAEL (CONT'D)
          ...the moment you return
          back home.

Galen scowls and thinks about it. He
finally lands on some stable idea. He
glances at Sofia who is placid and steady
as usual.

                    GALEN
          It doesn't matter. Nothing
          matters.

                    MICHAEL
          It matters if it matters.

Michael holds his hands up like a
telescope and peers at Galen through the
aperture. Galen points at him.

                    GALEN
          Perspective. Point of view.

                    MICHAEL
          Exactly.

Michael grins.

                    GALEN
          So now what?

                    MICHAEL
          He's testing you.

                    GALEN
          He has the entire world
          barnswaggled into believing
          him.

                    MICHAEL
          "Barnswaggled."

                    GALEN
     I don't understand! What am
     I supposed to do?

                    MICHAEL
     You're not "supposed" to do
     anything--

                    GALEN
               (interrupting)
     I know that! I'm not
     "supposed" to! I'm not
     "supposed" to do anything.
               (pause)
     Then what's the point?

Michael looks upon Galen. Galen blanches a
bit.

                    MICHAEL
     Free will...

Galen stares at Michael.

                    MICHAEL (CONT'D)
     ...means that it's up to
     you.
               (pause)
     It's ALL up to you.

Galen digests that. His hand reflexively
comes up and points to his chest.

And then he gets it. His eyes open and he
catches himself.

                    GALEN
     It's up to me...

Michael watches him closely. Galen looks
back at him.

                    GALEN (CONT'D)
     ...if I want to undo what
     he's created.

Michael and Sofia could be statues for
all that they give away to Galen. A cold
Icelandic breeze blows just in time as
Galen shudders and frowns.

                    GALEN (CONT'D)
          But I'm one of billions.
          It's not up to me.

Michael nods.

                    MICHAEL
          It's up to them too.

                    GALEN
          It's up to them!
                    (pause)
          It's up to me.

Slowly, a smile forms on Michael's face.
And he disappears.

Galen gapes where Michael had just been.

                    GALEN (CONT'D)
          Wait! Where'd he go?

Sofia shrugs, smiles.

                    GALEN (CONT'D)
          Was that...The Archangel?

She rolls her eyes.

                    SOFIA
          That's one term.

                    GALEN
          What is he?

                    SOFIA
          He's another spirit, a soul
          like you or me-

A ball of incandescent white light appears
adjacent to them, making Galen avert his

gaze and scrunch his eyes closed, hand up, warding it off. Sofia does the same until the light fades.

                    JEHOVAH
                  (booming)
          Galen, my son.

A bearded head, ten feet tall, is sitting in a fourth spot with them. JEHOVAH. No body, just flowing grey hair, and intense eyes.

Galen jumps when he opens his eyes and sees him. Sofia rolls her eyes.

JEHOVAH

You'll need my help.

Galen scowls at this creepy head. It's the face of an eighty-year-old man.

                    GALEN
          Who are you?

                    JEHOVAH
          I am that I am.

Galen blinks at him.

                    JEHOVAH
          I am your Lord. I am the
          Alpha and the Omega.

Sofia is still rolling her eyes.

                    JEHOVAH
          I am your one and only--

                    SOFIA
                  (interrupting)
          Save it, Yahwha!

Galen gapes at Sofia.

                    JEHOVAH
          I am--

                    SOFIA
                 (interrupting)
          He's just another
          spirit, another soul who
          hoodwinked a whole group
          of starving thirsty people
          into believing he was
          different from all of the
          other "gods" they found in
          the deserts and mountains
          and trees.

Galen continues gaping at her, periodically
checking in with Jehovah.

                    JEHOVAH
          I AM--

                    SOFIA
                 (interrupting)
          STOP!

Sofia looks at Galen and gestures as she
explains.

                    SOFIA (CONT'D)
          There's so much more to all
          of this than you know or
          have seen.
                 (pause)
          He's seen it. But he became
          a denser being.

Galen frowns.

                    SOFIA (CONT'D)
          The entire universe is made
          up of souls. You and I,
          Michael, Constantine, this
          guy.

She thumbs at Jehovah.

                    SOFIA (CONT'D)
          His real name is Yahwha,
          with some air in the "Yah"
          and the "chwah."
                    (pause)
          But nobody could pronounce
          it, hence the "YahWeh" and
          then "Jehovah."

Jehovah looks diminished. Galen is
dumbfounded.

                    SOFIA (CONT'D)
          Everyone's running about
          experiencing everything
          they can.
                    (pause)
          This one wanted to
          experience being "The ONE
          TRUE GOD."

She throws her hands up and rolls her eyes
yet again.

                    SOFIA (CONT'D)
          And he did a pretty
          convincing job.

She looks at Jehovah with a bit of
disdain.

                    SOFIA (CONT'D)
          Until the world started to
          forget him, distracted by
          that Jesus feller... And
          others.

Galen stares at Jehovah.

                    JEHOVAH
          You need my help if you're
          going to defeat this
          upstart Constantine.

Galen listens and then...

                    GALEN
          You've had two thousand
          years to do something
          about him.

Jehovah takes umbrage but stops short.

Galen gets an idea. Jehovah regroups and
attempts to say something.

                    GALEN (CONT'D)
          NO! You've benefitted from
          the same falsehood...

Galen FLASHES to Noah and the Flood, Sodom
and Gomorrah, and the Plagues upon Egypt...

                    GALEN (CONT'D)
          ...and oceans of blood.

Galen looks angry. Jehovah freezes. He
glances around...

...and disappears.

                    SOFIA
          Nice.

Galen contemplates what just happened.

                    GALEN
          Will that work on
          Constantine?

                    SOFIA
          Dunno.
                    (pause)
          He's kept up the ruse more
          effectively. It's pretty
          brilliant. Instead of
          trying to prove he's God,
          focusing on himself, he's
          focused everyone on reality
          itself, proving how hard
          life is and how much you
                    (MORE)

                    SOFIA (CONT'D)
          all need divine intervention.

Galen listens intently.

                    SOFIA (CONT'D)
          "Death and taxes."

Galen stands up and paces, periodically
distracted by the Icelandic tundra and cold
wind.

                    GALEN
          Gravity. Hot and cold.
          Right and wrong.
          Conservative and liberal.
          North and South, East and
          West.

A cold gust gets his attention and he
shivers.

                    GALEN (CONT'D)
          Why did you choose this
          place?

                    SOFIA
          I thought of the Moon, but
          I figured that would freak
          you out too much.

Galen nods appreciatively.

EXT. TAHITI - DUSK

On a beach sitting in lounge chairs.

                    SOFIA
          Better?

Galen does a double-take at their beautiful
new surroundings. He's speechless for a
moment.

He looks at her and thinks some more.

                    GALEN
          If I want to undo what
          Constantine has done,
          I need to...pry so many
          people from their...
          delusion.

Sofia considers that.

                    SOFIA
          People who believe in this
          reality?

He nods.

                    SOFIA (CONT'D)
          How many is that?

Galen looks up.

                    GALEN
          Eight point two billion?
          Give or take?

Sofia laughs.

                    SOFIA
          That's a lot of convincing.

Galen is stricken by the challenge.

Something on the ocean catches his
attention. He stands up and peers out,
trying to see what it is.

                    GALEN
          What is that?

Sofia glances.

                    SOFIA
          Oh. That's garbage.

Galen glances across the panorama of the
ocean. A huge garbage patch floats not too
far off into the ocean, ruining what was a
beautiful view.

                    GALEN
          Garbage?

Those red streaks reach their skies along
with distant TRUMPET BLARES, each one
getting closer, louder.

Some Tahitians nearby CRY out and MURMUR
prayers in anguish.

Sofia and Galen look at them and then each
other.

                    SOFIA
          Thoughts?

INT. HOSPITAL ROOM

Allie is being helped to the bathroom by a
nurse.

Trayvon is at the window, looking out
nervously. The TRUMPET BLARES are clear,
loud, and frightening.

INT. CNN NEWS STAGE

Wolf Blitzer is in the middle of a segment.
Galen is now sitting adjacent to him at the
news desk.

                    WOLF BLITZER
          ...per the report- WHAT THE
          FUCK?!? Oh, God! Shit!

He jumps from his seat and almost falls
down. He regains his balance, hears
something in his ear piece, scans the
studio, and focuses on Galen.

                    WOLF BLITZER (CONT'D)
          My apologies! My deepest
          apologies! I was caught off
          guard.

He climbs back onto his seat and gulps
for air as he tries to compose himself. He
pauses a moment and focuses on Galen with
an anxious smile.

                    WOLF BLITZER (CONT'D)
          It's you! Welcome. How did
          you... Never mind that.
                    (muttering)
          Clearly you can...
                    (re-focused)
          Thank you for joining us.

Galen smiles and uncertainly looks at the
various cameras. He finds his and smiles
more intentionally at the viewers.

                    GALEN
          Thank you.

Wolf Blitzer pauses and calculates an idea.

                    WOLF BLITZER
          Who? No... What...what are
          you...here. Why...are you--

                    GALEN
                    (interrupting)
          I'm just here to share
          with...everyone...that
          this...

Galen gestures towards everything...

                    GALEN (CONT'D)
          ...is not what we assume it
          is.

                    WOLF BLITZER
          "This?" The world?

                    GALEN
          Reality.

                    WOLF BLITZER
          "Reality."

                    GALEN
          Correct.

He looks into his camera again, smiling
for emphasis.

                    WOLF BLITZER
          Then...what is it?

Galen thinks.

                    GALEN
          Well...suffice it to say
          that we assume way too
          much about this reality.

                    WOLF BLITZER
          Assume...
                    (pause)
          An assumption is...

He checks with his producers; he's being
fed information.

                    WOLF BLITZER (CONT'D)
          Um, an assumption is "a
          thing that is accepted...
          as true...or as certain to
          happen,...without proof.

Galen thinks and nods happily.

                    GALEN
          That works.

                    WOLF BLITZER
          Are you saying that we
          need proof, proof that we
          don't have?

Galen smiles.

                    GALEN
          I don't think I can say
          much more...that would be
          really helpful.

Wolf Blitzer gapes at him.

                    GALEN (CONT'D)
          The question perhaps is
          more useful, more powerful.

The huge monitors on the set cut to
video from around the world of fire and
brimstone, people in anguish, crying,
running up to cameras, storms brewing
with strange red clouds, and the TRUMPET
BLARES.

                    WOLF BLITZER
          We're cutting back to our
          feeds from around the
          world. Do you see this? Are
          you aware of this?

Galen looks at the video feeds carefully
and nods. He looks at Blitzer.

                    WOLF BLITZER (CONT'D)
              (distraught)
          What are we assuming about
          that? That's happening!
          That's REAL! Isn't it?

Galen tilts his head.

                    GALEN
          You saw me before when I
          exposed that...being. You
          saw that too. Right?

Wolf Blitzer gulps and scowls. He's having
a real hard time dealing with these recent
events. Tears brim in his eyes. He stares
at his script pages.

                    WOLF BLITZER
          God says that Judgment day
          is coming and we will all
          be judged for our sins.
          Judgment day...

He looks up at Galen, tears fall.

                    WOLF BLITZER (CONT'D)
          ...seems to be here, now!

He stares at Galen. Galen stares back
empathically.

                    GALEN
          Does "God" say that?

Blitzer stammers, splutters.

                    WOLF BLITZER
          It's in the Bible! It's--

                    GALEN
               (interrupting)
          And that's "God" saying
          that?

                    WOLF BLITZER
               (angry)
          It's the WORD of GOD!

Galen looks at him compassionately.

                    GALEN
          There are two laws in the
          Universe, Love and Free
          Will.

Blitzer is wiping his tears with his hands.
An assistant delivers a box of tissues.
Blitzer is not angry so much as scared,
terrified even. He snatches some tissues
and mutters an apology.

                    WOLF BLITZER
               (sniffling)
          Love and free will...

                    GALEN
          Yes. Where is Judgment in
          that?

Blitzer blinks in confusion. He wipes his face vigorously and looks at Galen, studying him.

                    WOLF BLITZER
          Love and free will...have
          no judgment.

                    GALEN
          Not the "punishment" you
          mean. Not the retribution.

Galen seems to recall his own guilt. He looks at Wolf Blitzer with a smile.

Blitzer struggles to understand.

                    WOLF BLITZER
          What is Love?

Galen rocks back a bit. He pauses, thinking.

                    GALEN
          That's an excellent
          question.
                    (pause)
          I think I'm still learning
          the answer.

Blitzer nods.

                    GALEN (CONT'D)
          Well, it's too simple to
          think of it as just an
          emotion.
                    (pause)
          I think...it's more like a
          glue.

                    WOLF BLITZER
          Glue?!? Love is a glue.

                    GALEN
          Love holds everything
          together.

Blitzer turns away, thinking.

                    GALEN (CONT'D)
          Hate, hate is a fire. It
          causes cancer, it burns
          out, and it doesn't hold
          things together for very
          long.
                    (pause)
          Hate is brittle and
          immediate. Love is flexible
          and...eternal.
                    (pause)
          If the Universe were built
          on hate, it would have
          collapsed thirty minutes
          after the Big Bang.

Wolf Blitzer stares at Galen, pursing his
lips, thinking, hand to his mouth.

Assistant producers rush in with the
Priest, Imam, and Rabbi from previous
segments and seat them awkwardly at the
table, finalizing their mics and earpieces.

A FEMALE ASSISTANT tentatively hands Galen
his mic and earpiece. He looks at them,
unsure what to do. She nervously clips the
mic to his coat's lapel and hands him the
earpiece.

He checks it, hears something that makes
him start a bit, and decides to hold it in
his lap instead.

                    GALEN (CONT'D)
          Can you hear me now?

                    WOLF BLITZER
          Yes, it's fine. It's better.
                    (pause)
          We're joined by our religious
          consultants who I'm sure
          have many questions.

Galen smiles at all of them and looks the clerics over.

                    GALEN
          I have one question.

Blitzer is pleasantly surprised.

                    WOLF BLITZER
          By all means.

Galen gestures with a hand and a smile at the clerics.

                    GALEN
          Where are the women?

Blitzer and the clerics are stumped by the question. Blitzer looks off-stage to his producers, nodding at them. He turns to Galen.

                    WOLF BLITZER
          Gentlemen? I think our
          guest is...pointing out an
          assumption, another one
          perhaps.

Nervous smiles flit across the clerics faces. The Rabbi holds up a dismissive hand.

                    RABBI
          Who are you?

Galen nods at him.

                    GALEN
          My name is Galen.

                    RABBI
          What are you? How...did you
          come about to...

                    GALEN
          I...am a man. I was a
          priest, long ago. And...a
          lot has happened to me.

                    WOLF BLITZER
          You're a priest!

                    GALEN
          I was. No longer.

                    WOLF BLITZER
          Why is that? If I may ask.

                    GALEN
          That's a longer story that
          wouldn't help all of you,
          all of us right now.

                    PRIEST
          What would help us now?

Galen looks at them.

                    GALEN
          Question your assumptions
          about this reality.

Galen looks at his camera and smiles.

                    IMAM
          Question!

                    GALEN (CONT'D)
          Don't assume so readily
          that what is happening
          is...all there is.

The video feeds change abruptly. Calamities
that were happening suddenly stop or
disappear, like Satan and Armageddon had
done.

All on set notice.

                    WOLF BLITZER
          We seem to have some
          developments.

Other than Galen, they all check with each
other, confused. The production staff put
up a grid of news feeds from more places.

Each one shows a stoppage or complete
disappearance of the disturbance that
was happening. The anguished people in
the streets look around, dumbfounded and
relieved.

Blitzer holds a hand to his mouth. He
turns to Galen and drops his hand.

                    WOLF BLITZER (CONT'D)
          Is that your doing?

Galen smiles, abashedly. He glances at the
clerics and enthusiastically shakes his
head.

                    GALEN
          No.

                    WOLF BLITZER
          But it looks like it's
          stopping again. Is this
          real? You didn't do this?

Galen looks at the screens, smiling.

                    GALEN
          No.

He looks into his camera...

                    GALEN (CONT'D)
          You're doing this.

...and at Blitzer who looks around,
dumbfounded. He studies his monitors and
the news feeds. Some of his tension is
released and he GIGGLES, CHUCKLES, and

then LAUGHS. The clerics exhale a SIGH of
relief.

                    WOLF BLITZER
          We're getting reports of...
          cessations of these various
          frightening events from all
          around the world.

A bigger screen pushes the smaller feeds
into a new layout. The shot is of a
harried FOREIGN CORRESPONDENT.

                    CORRESPONDENT
                    (shouting)
          Yes. We're seeing what
          can only be described as
          a miracle. These jets,
          columns of flames from the
          ground have just stopped
          and the streets are...
          healing themselves.

                    WOLF BLITZER
          Where are you reporting
          from?

                    GALEN
          Thank you.

Galen steps off his seat and sets his mic
and ear piece on the news desk.

And disappears.

                    WOLF BLITZER
          Wait! Where?

Blitzer reacts to Galen's disappearance.
The Clerics just look like three of the
apostles in DaVinci's The Last Supper,
startled.

EXT. NEW YORK CITY STREET

A reporter is interviewing a MAN (30). He's
flustered but happy, recently crying.

                    MAN
          I mean, it's the fucking
          end of the world! I was
          distraught.
                    (pause)
          But then that guy,
          Scarf Guy. When he said
          "Question." It just popped
          in my head. Like a zit!
                    (pause)
          This concrete painful thing
          I believed one thousand
          percent...suddenly split in
          half and...collapsed.

WOMAN 2 (45) is being interviewed, face wet
with tears.

                    WOMAN 2
          It just...went away. Like
          waking up from a nightmare.
          "Wait a second. What if
          it's not true...?"

An OLD MAN (75) is being interviewed, tears
are still streaming down his face, but
he's overjoyed. He looks around, gesturing,
almost dancing.

                    OLD MAN
          My whole life...and
          suddenly, maybe it's not
          real?!?

He smiles at the reporter and then the
camera.

                    OLD MAN
          What a relief...

MONTAGE Around the world.

In cities and remote villages people are looking into the skies with relief, some clutching each other happily, tears are flowing. Smiles and laughter permeates these various moments.

The red skies slip away into nothingness. Terrifying cracks in the ground heal and where there was fire and brimstone it has all cleared away.

The world is back to normal.

At the hospital, Trayvon is in the hallway talking to a doctor. Allie is watching the news and looking out the window, smiling.
End MONTAGE

EXT. STREET/CNN BUILDING

Galen pops onto the sidewalk but no one notices him suddenly appearing there. He steps out, looking up at the buildings and the clearing skies. Most people are torn between looking up and getting to their destinations.

                    BISHOP
          There you are!

Galen looks and sees the Bishop who approaches him anxiously. He extends his hands and takes Galen's in a handshake. Galen complies, going along.

                    GALEN
          Excellency...

                    BISHOP
          Galen?

Galen nods and smiles at him.

                    BISHOP
          I was hoping I could find you.
          I have so many questions.

                    GALEN (CONT'D)
          Really?

The Bishop suddenly becomes Constantine,
now in a gaudy Versace suit, but he wears
it comfortably, rather than it wearing him.

                    CONSTANTINE
          Actually one. What are you
          doing?

Galen steps back.

                    GALEN
          What are you doing?

Constantine has no patience for this
miscreant and snaps his fingers.

They disappear and only the Homeless Guy,
from before, notices them go.

INT. CATHEDRAL

The cathedral is empty. Galen and
Constantine appear in the crossing, facing
off.

                    GALEN
                 (scowling)
          While love is the fabric
          of the universe, you've
          created so much hate and
          misery...

Galen paces in front of Constantine who
shakes his head at this naive child.

                    CONSTANTINE
          Exactly.

Galen stops sand stares at him.

                    GALEN
          What?!?

Constantine is exultant, not so much smiling as nearly orgasmic.

                    CONSTANTINE
          Love...

Constantine seems to expect Galen to understand from that one word. Galen has no patience for this narcissist.

                    GALEN
          What ABOUT IT?!?

                    CONSTANTINE
          Did you love Sofia, Galen
          Brand? Or were you just
          fucking her?

Galen is taken aback, perplexed. He looks at Constantine hostilely.

                    CONSTANTINE (CONT'D)
               (teasing)
          Was it just sex guilt that
          made you hang yourself?
          Ooh, "the temptation of the
          flesh"?

Galen FLASHES back to his abject weeping, kneeling on the grass, clutching the rope he's found. Sobbing and slobbering, he ties a noose.

                    CONSTANTINE (CONT'D)
               (serious)
          Or was it something else?

Constantine peers at him, piercingly, doggedly, knowingly. Galen winces, revisiting that pain. He drops to his knees on the marble floor, staring into the past.

                    GALEN
          I...I...LOVED her!

                    CONSTANTINE
          Yesss...! And wasn't
          that just unimaginably
          beautiful?!?

He's thrust forward his hands as if
fondling reality in the most carnal way
possible. Galen notices and snaps out of
it.

He stands up, shakes his head, glowering.

                    GALEN
          Beautiful?

Constantine stares at him expectantly, like
an insane teacher with his most traumatized
student.

                    GALEN (CONT'D)
          You think my love was made
          greater...by that horrendous
          heartache?!?
                    (pause)
          She was burnt ALIVE, YOU
          MOTHERFUCKER!

Galen rushes into his face, spittle and
tears flying. Constantine is eating it up.

                    GALEN (CONT'D)
          By your FUCKING CHURCH!

Constantine relishes the emotion, closing
his eyes post-orgasmically.

                    CONSTANTINE
          Utter and complete
          clarity...

He opens his eyes and gazes at Galen.
Constantine pinches his fingers...

                    CONSTANTINE (CONT'D)
          Not one angstrom of doubt!

...demonstrating his poINT. Galen glares back, starting to understand.

                    CONSTANTINE (CONT'D)
          Pure...Love...

Galen blinks and straightens up. He steps back, whirls, a hand on his hip, a hand to his forehead. He turns and faces Constantine with a look of...clarity.

                    GALEN
          All of this...

Constantine gazes upon him, so close to triumph.

                    GALEN (CONT'D)
          ...is about love...?

Constantine closes his eyes, clutches his heart like an unctuous Bishop with a virginal maiden he's blessed, smiling.

Galen just watches him.

                    CONSTANTINE
          ...yes.

He opens his eyes and is surprised to see Galen's lack of agreement.

                    GALEN
          And you? Do you have that
          love right now?

Galen dramatically spins around, indicating the lack of any love interest for Constantine.

                    CONSTANTINE
          I...

His face twitches as his triumph falters. He shakes his head at the naivete again.

                    CONSTANTINE (CONT'D)
          It's...greater than just
          one...

He gestures at the ephemeral.

Galen peers at him.

                    GALEN
          I'll take that as a "No."

Constantine scowls at Galen's reductivism.

                    CONSTANTINE
                    (lecturing)
          You have no idea--

                    GALEN
                    (interrupting)
          All of those souls...were
          content with love.

Constantine stops speaking.

                    GALEN (CONT'D)
          They didn't have to...
          smear...all this...SHIT...

Constantine blinks.

                    GALEN (CONT'D)
          ...to super charge the
          experience.
                    (pause)
          You child...

Constantine sneers.

                    GALEN (CONT'D)
          Well, it's over! You're
          done!

Constantine watches him.

                    GALEN (CONT'D)
          Your big show has been
          revealed to your believers.

Constantine thinks and nods slightly. He
frowns, conceding a poINT.

                    CONSTANTINE
          My believers, perhaps.

Galen continues to glare at him.

                    CONSTANTINE (CONT'D)
          But I have others.

Galen frowns.

                    GALEN
          What others?

Constantine plants himself squarely,
holding his hands.

                    CONSTANTINE
          I tried religion.
                    (pause)
          Now I'm going to try
          something more fundamental.

Constantine disappears, leaving Galen
scowling alone. He looks around to no
avail.

EXT. VERANDA, ROMAN PALACE, 326 A.D.
(FLASHBACK)

Constantine, in his Emperor's garb, gazes
at Constantinople on three sides.

Behind him, HELENA (70), Constantine's
mother, leans on one of two tables, each
with a shrouded body, one a man and the
other clearly a woman.

                    HELENA
          Do you know nothing of love?!?

Constantine smiles, almost laughs. Helena's tears are flowing. She clutches the foot of the male corpse.

> HELENA (CONT'D)
> You killed my grandson before confirming the rumors?

She gestures to the female corpse.

> HELENA (CONT'D)
> And now this?
> (pause)
> Are you insane?

Constantine FLASHES back to a shared kiss with his wife FAUSTA, 15 years younger than him.

Still facing the city, hiding from Helena's scorn, Constantine's face struggles between a forlorn smile and a maniacal look of shame as his tears also flow freely. End FLASHBACK

EXT. SPACE

The sun is blazing. A burst of light emerges from it, a solar burp.

EXT. MERCURY - DAY

This planet is a vista of volcanic rock. Stars shine in the sky with the sun in view given its thin atmosphere.

The sun noticeably grows, expanding. More burps or bursts of energy emerge from the star.

What's left of Mercury's atmosphere gets thinner as the sun grows even more.

INT. COMMERCIAL AIRLINER - DAY

The CO-PILOT, sunglasses on, is facing forward, flying west over the cloud cover. He sees one of the bursts of energy.

                    CO-PILOT
          What was that?

The Pilot looks up from the checklist she was annotating.

                    PILOT
          Oh, yeah. I noticed
          something.

                    CO-PILOT
          There was a burst of light.

She looks around the cockpit, checking lights.

                    PILOT
          Was that in here?

                    CO-PILOT
          No...

The Pilot looks at her Co-Pilot and then out the windshields, slipping her sunglasses down from her head.

Another light burst happens.

                    PILOT
          Whoa! Is that what you
          meant?

                    CO-PILOT
          Yeah...

                    PILOT
          How many times did it--

Another burst happens.

                    PILOT
          What the...?
                    (pause)
          Center. U.A. Three-four-
          seven, reporting an
          anomaly.

                    ATC
                    (filtered)
          United three-four-seven,
          roger. What's the issue?

EXT. INTERNATIONAL SPACE STATION

An astronaut, HICKENLOOPER (48), is floating
at a computer station in a brightly lit
cylindrical section of the station.

The array has four monitors in a quad.
One of them has the sun centered with data
streaming on the side. The other monitors
have histograms and other information
playing out.

                    HICKENLOOPER
          That's not right.

She flips around and propels herself to
the nearest intersection.

VIEWPORT

Hickenlooper swims hand-over-hand to
an octagonal window structure. Another
astronaut, SINGH (33), is there, looking at
the sun. He grabs some goggles velcro'ed to
the bulkhead and dons them.

                    HICKENLOOPER
          Singh, what's the sun
          doing?

                    SINGH
          Why do you ask?

                    HICKENLOOPER
          My measurements are going
          crazy, like it's...

                    SINGH
          ...brightening?

She grabs another pair of goggles and puts
them on. They're made of very dark neutral-
density filters specifically for viewing
the sun.

                    HICKENLOOPER
          That's definitely not right.

INT. CNN NEWS STAGE

Wolf Blitzer is still reporting on events
around the world.

                    WOLF BLITZER
          By all accounts things have
          settled down, miraculously
          some are saying.
                    (pause)
          We're cutting to a new item
          coming across our desk...

The monitors behind him cut to the White
House press briefing room.

The White House PRESS SECRETARY (39) a
blonde woman steps behind the lectern in
what feels like a hastily called briefing.
Even CNN's camera has to adjust their shot.

                    PRESS SECRETARY
          We've received reports from
          the ISS, the International
          Space Station and the White
          House's science center of
          a strange anomaly they're
          noticing with the sun.

INT. WHITE HOUSE BRIEFING ROOM

The assembled members of the presidential
administration seem nervous. The reporters
are still finding their seats and settling
in.

                    PRESS SECRETARY (CONT'D)
          NASA is reporting that
          the sun has increased in
          brightness in the last
          three hours, a five percent
          increase according to some
          estimates. Scientists are
          still trying to figure out
          why this has happened. As
          you can guess, staring at
          the sun is not an easy
          task.

INT. CNN NEWS STAGE - CONTINUOUS

Wolf Blitzer looks like he can't take
much more news. The religious clerics are
still with him at the desk with fearful
expressions on their faces. An Episcopalian
FEMALE PRIEST has been added to the panel
since the last time.

INSERT: The chyron on the monitors reads,
"Anmaly with the Earth's Sun." The typo
instantly gets corrected.

                    PRESS SECRETARY (CONT'D)
                    (on-screen)
          Given recent spectacular
          events the White House
          decided to release this
          information immediately.
          Experts, as I said, are
          still trying to figure out
          the cause of, what they're
          calling "sun bursts".

INT. TAHITI - NIGHT

Galen is with Sofia at their resort
bungalow watching the news. Galen looks
worried. Sofia is matter-of-fact about it
all. She looks at him.

                    PRESS SECRETARY (CONT'D)
                (on TV)
          We're told that sun
          bursts do happen, from
          time to time, but these
          are different in nature.
          There is no definitive
          information beyond that. We
          will update you as soon as
          more details come in.

Wolf Blitzer turns to the assembled
clerics.

                    WOLF BLITZER
                (on TV)
          Joining us is Mother Irene
          Fogelson representing the
          Episcopal Church. Mother,
          what are your immediate
          thoughts regarding this
          announcement?

MOTHER FOGELSON (45) looks ill.

                    MOTHER FOGELSON
                (on TV)
          It's a lot to digest, Wolf.
          Thank you for having me
          on your panel. As the
          secretary said we'll have
          to wait for developments.

                    WOLF BLITZER
          Do you think this is part
          of Armageddon, perhaps a
          third phase?

                    MOTHER FOGELSON
          Right now there are no
          indications that's the
          case. But it's been an
          eventful few days.

She looks at the other clerics who also
look ill at ease.

                    GALEN
          He just said he was going
          to try "something more
          fundamental."

Sofia mutes the TV.

                    GALEN (CONT'D)
          He tried religion...

He looks at Sofia, concerned.

                    GALEN (CONT'D)
          He's showing off by making
          the sun brighter. That
          should scare them...

He rushes to their balcony and goes
outside. The night sky is not affected,
yet. But the moon is much brighter and
the surroundings are easier to see. Galen
squints at the moon.

Sofia joins him and notices the brightness.

                    GALEN (CONT'D)
          If he can do that, why
          didn't he just stick with
          Armageddon?

He turns to Sofia. She thinks about the
situation.

                    SOFIA
          He's working with what's
          available.

Galen comes back inside and plops into one of their comfy chairs.

                    SOFIA (CONT'D)
          This reality has been
          around for quite a long
          time.

Galen looks at her.

                    GALEN
          How long?

                    SOFIA
          Billions of years.

                    GALEN
          So he didn't create this?
          But he created Armageddon?

                    SOFIA
          He's manipulating what all
          of us believe.

                    GALEN
          Believe.

                    SOFIA
          Billions of religious
          people believed in the End
          of the World.

Galen nods.

                    GALEN
          But billions more believe
          in...the Sun. The Earth,
          the Moon... I think I get
          it.

                    SOFIA
          It's like layers of beliefs.

He looks at her.

                    GALEN
          You keep saying "us."
          You're including yourself
          with us mere mortals?

She chuckles.

                    SOFIA
          I'm human, at least in this
          iteration, just like you.

                    GALEN
          But aren't you...elevated?

                    SOFIA
          I am.

                    GALEN
          How?

                    SOFIA
          It's a very long story.

He gazes at her, not letting her off the
hook.

                    SOFIA (CONT'D)
          I've been presented with
          opportunities to come back
          to...this many times and I
          took them. You don't forget
          those and it opens up a
          lot of other memories. A
          lot.

Galen slouches deeper into his chair,
contemplating her. He smiles, taken by her
beauty.

                    GALEN
          And you keep coming back.

                    SOFIA
          It's one of the best games
          in town.

                    GALEN
          Are you back?!?

                    SOFIA
          Correct. I'm like you right
          now. Sort of in-between.

                    GALEN
          In between gigs?

                    SOFIA
          Going through the terrible
          twos and high school again
          is rough...

                    GALEN
          Worse than the sun
          brightening?

                    SOFIA
          The sun's growing.

He does a double-take and looks at Sofia.

MONTAGE AROUND THE WORLD.

The sun becomes brighter. Visible rings
expand from it at irregular intervals.

The sky is a hazy lighter blue. In a city
somewhere in the world people look up in
wonder and fear. A YOUNG MAN shades his
eyes but then screams as he realizes that
he can't see. Then he clutches his eyes in
pain.

THE ARCTIC CIRCLE The icecaps melt, fall
apart much faster than any documentary
has shown. The calving has given over to
actual melting.

New York, London, and Tokyo are submerged
by relentless large waves moving inland.

THE SAHARA, LIBYA People cower under any
structure. Livestock die on the spot from

the heat. Even indoors is insufferable.

BRITISH COLUMBIA Forests erupt into colossal firestorms, spreading as fast as hurricanes.

OBSERVATORY Astronomers and astrophysicists, trying to stay cool in their labs, watch data stream in on their computers.

> ASTRONOMER 1
> Mercury is about to be
> absorbed.

The rest of the astronomers standing by collectively gulp.

> ASTRONOMER 1
> That happened approximately
> eight minutes ago.

HOSPITAL DELIVERY ROOM

Allie is in labor, Trayvon is in scrubs and helping her breathe. The BIRTH TEAM is busy and focused. End MONTAGE

EXT. SPACE

Galen and Sofia, dressed as usual, are floating in space. Galen freaks out.

> GALEN
> What is going on?

> SOFIA
> Relax!

Galen realizes that he's not falling and doesn't really have to do anything to keep from falling. Sofia calmly floats in space.

They have a vantage point of Earth, which appears relatively small from this distance, and they observe the Sun slowly expanding.

                    MICHAEL
          It's quite a spectacle.

Galen turns to...

                    GALEN
          Michael! What can we do?

Eleven more beings, like Michael, appear
floating in space. Some look human, others
are humanoid but blue or onyx black.

Galen gazes at a blue being and can swear
that he's looking at ENKI as he looks like
all of the Sumerian carvings he's seen.

INT. CONFERENCE ROOM

It's a sleek retro, 1960s conference room
with one wall of windows looking out at
the view of the Earth and the Sun.

All of the 14 assembled beings are sitting
at this large mahogany table. Most are
taller than Galen and Sofia, even seated.

                    ENKI
          This has gone too far.

Michael nods. The other enlightened beings
look at each other and nod.

                    SOFIA
          Then we summon him.

                    MICHAEL
          Indeed.

Michael gestures with one hand.

Constantine in a different Versace suit
appears, standing in the middle of the
table. He's surprised to suddenly be there
and whirls around.

He gazes at the different beings, finally
resting on Galen.

                    CONSTANTINE
          You...

He straightens up and spins around,
acknowledging the rest.

                    CONSTANTINE (CONT'D)
          What do you want?

                    MICHAEL
          You're destroying the
          planet.

                    INANNA
          That seems extreme.

Constantine turns to INANNA, the Sumerian
goddess. She is one potent embodiment of
sex and sexiness even though she's deadly
serious at the moment.

                    CONSTANTINE
          Jehovah did that a few
          times.

Inanna rolls her eyes at the waste of
lives.

                    CONSTANTINE (CONT'D)
          What do you care?
                    (pause)
          You all have other...
          projects! You have your own
          hobbies to entertain you.

                    INANNA
          You're imposing your will
          on billions.

Constantine gesticulates with a flourish.

                    CONSTANTINE
          They've all chosen it!

                    GALEN
          Liar.

Constantine glares at Galen. The assembled
look at Galen as well. Sofia calmly watches
Galen.

Constantine, on the table, steps closer to
Galen and looks down at him. Galen sits up
not used to these encounters.

                    CONSTANTINE
          I am many things, but not
          a liar.

                    GALEN
          Lies. You've lied for so
          long, you don't recognize
          that your very existence is
          a lie.

                    CONSTANTINE
          They've all chosen these
          lives, these experiences.
          They know--

                    GALEN
               (interrupting)
          They chose!

                    CONSTANTINE
          Yes!

Constantine nods at him confidently.

                    GALEN
          Can they choose to not die
          from the expanding sun?
          Can they "opt out" of this
          cataclysm? They all have
          other things they'd rather
          be doing.

Galen looks around the table. All of the
exalted beings are listening closely, even
the amorphous energy being.

He checks in with Sofia who is gazing at him admiringly. That surprises him and then reminds him of something.

                    GALEN (CONT'D)
          You!

Galen points at Constantine and snaps his fingers.

INT. CNN NEWS STAGE

Wolf Blitzer is drawing a segment to a close.

                    WOLF BLITZER
          Next up we'll have
          continuing coverage of
          world events as more--oh
          fuck!

Galen and Constantine have popped onto the set, standing in front of the news desk.

                    WOLF BLITZER (CONT'D)
          Not again...
                    (pause)
          We're having a new
          development as we speak.
          I hope I'm not the only
          one seeing this, but our
          previous guest, Galen, whom
          you all recall from the
          dramatic moments in the
          Negev desert and someone
          else.

Constantine looks around, smirking. The stage crew scramble to line up boom mics over Constantine and Galen.

                    GALEN
          Almost all of the world
          is listening, watching us
          right now.

Constantine chuckles at Galen's theatrics.

                    CONSTANTINE
          Screw this...

He points at Galen.

                    CONSTANTINE (CONT'D)
          What's that in your hand?

Galen looks. Incongruously, he's holding the ROPE he used to hang himself.

EXT. FARM - MORNING

Galen is his biracial self, looking down, but back as a priest in the past.

He's holding a chubby BABY, which startles him. But he doesn't drop him. The Baby has Galen's blue eyes and Sofia's complexion.

Galen looks up and Sofia is standing, not too far away, with their DAUGHTER who is clutching her mother's leg. He looks around at their modest farm, smiling.

Galen looks back down at his baby as he cradles him, grinning. His expression changes...

                    GALEN
          No... NO!

...as he realizes what this is.

The Baby flashes fear on his face, then starts CRYING.

                    GALEN (CONT'D)
                 (yelling)
          NOOO!

The farm, baby, Sofia, and the 1400s get sucked away to blackness as Galen scrunches his eyes closed, YELLING.

Galen points generally where Constantine had been standing.

He SNAPS his fingers.

The darkness reveals Constantine, in his Versace suit, surprised.

                    CONSTANTINE
          How did you...

He locks with Galen's angry gaze.

                    GALEN
          Leave them ALONE...

Galen stares Constantine down. Constantine has been in countless battles and done who knows what, but Galen is different.

Galen snaps his fingers in Constantine's face.

EXT. NEGEB DESERT - DAWN

Constantine rocks on his heels, looks around.

The sun has not risen over the horizon yet, but the sky is brighter than normal.

A portion of the CNN news studio has appeared in the desert, fully functional with the production staff scrambling to figure out what just happened to them.

Around Constantine, one-by-one other portions of news desks appear in this spot of land, from India, South America, China, Japan, France, England, Africa.

Constantine is intrigued.

A circle of eight or more TV production sets are magically in the Palestinian desert.

As the professionals they all are, the NEWS DIRECTORS and ANCHORS focus on Constantine and Galen, incongruously standing in the desert sand as the wind whips through.

Galen steps out to what looks like the center. He can see himself on monitors in the various "sets."

Hapless Wolf Blitzer is there, interacting with his production team.

                    GALEN (CONT'D)
          Wolf. Mr. Blitzer. Can you
          hear me?
                    (pause)
          Can you all hear me?

He gets an assortment of thumbs-ups from all around.

                    WOLF BLITZER
          Yes, Galen. We can hear
          you.

                    GALEN
          Constantine. Emperor. Would
          you like to introduce
          yourself?

Galen gestures to the TV crews surrounding them. Constantine is not amused anymore. He was not expecting this. He actually clasps his hands behind his back and paces.

                    CONSTANTINE
          Get on with it, Priest.

Galen checks with Wolf Blitzer and gestures to his ear. Blitzer nods and thumbs up.

                    GALEN
          The Earth's Sun is
          expanding.

Blitzer gapes at him uncertainly. The various on-set monitors and video walls show calamities of unimagined scales occurring around the world.

                    GALEN (CONT'D)
          What you see in the sky
          happened eight minutes ago.

Constantine scowls at Galen.

                    GALEN (CONT'D)
          This...

He gestures to Constantine. Constantine pauses his pacing, uncertain.

                    GALEN (CONT'D)
          Is the man responsible for
          all of this...hurt.

Galen jabs his finger at CNN's video monitor behind Wolf Blitzer and archival footage and images of Constantine the Great show up, including the phrase "In Hoc Signo Vinces."

Constantine purses his lips in annoyance and anger.

                    GALEN (CONT'D)
          You know him as the last
          Roman Emperor and basically
          the first Pope!

Galen steps forward dramatically, waving his arms.

                    GALEN (CONT'D)
          He accepted and converted
          to Christianity from
          his evil pagan ways and
          solidified the Eastern
          Roman Empire which became
          the Roman Catholic Church.

Galen turns to all of the assorted cameras trained on him, almost like a rockstar on stage.

                    GALEN (CONT'D)
          And two THOUSAND years
          of genocide, brutality,
          persecution, and bloodlust
          later.

Galen steps up to Wolf Blitzer.

                    GALEN (CONT'D)
          You all believe that this
          is...The End of the World.

Blitzer attempts to say something, ask something. But he can't.

Galen smiles at him in a forlorn way. He turns to the other cameras, giving them the same treatment.

Galen turns to Constantine and gestures to him.

                    GALEN (CONT'D)
          What...say...you...?

Constantine gulps slightly. He looks around, annoyed but composed. He chooses to close the distance between himself and Galen.

                    CONSTANTINE
          What do you think you're
          accomplishing here, Priest?

                    GALEN
          Galen.

Constantine sneers slightly.

                    CONSTANTINE
          Galen Brand.

He turns to the cameras.

                    CONSTANTINE (CONT'D)
          Galen Brand, everybody. A
          big hand for Galen Brand!
                    (pause)
          Philandering priest,
          suicide, cursed to hell,
          loser.

Galen stares at Constantine, unimpressed.

He turns to Wolf Blitzer.

                    GALEN
          Mr. Blitzer.

                    WOLF BLITZER
          Wolf.

                    GALEN
          Wolf. Do you think the
          world should end?

Galen waits patiently. Blitzer feels
suddenly on the spot, but then seems to
remember that the question is very simple
as is the answer...

                    WOLF BLITZER
          No!

Galen paces dramatically, crossing in front
of Constantine and glancing at him. He
turns to look at Blitzer.

                    GALEN
          Why not?

Blitzer gapes at him and splutters. He
composes himself, looking around at his
colleagues from around the world (some he's
met).

He looks uneasily at Constantine and then
at Galen.

                    WOLF BLITZER
          We're not done yet.

Galen stops, punctuating his answer.

                    GALEN
          You're "not done yet."

He looks at Constantine.

                    GALEN (CONT'D)
          You're not done with what
          yet?

Blitzer splutters some more, but quickly
composes himself and formulates a response.

                    WOLF BLITZER
          We're not done with our...
          potential. Yet.

Blitzer is suddenly more secure, stable
standing next to Constantine. Galen turns
to face him.

                    GALEN
          Your potential for what?

Blitzer takes his time now, looking around,
breathing, and really contemplating the
question. He looks at both Galen and
Constantine.

                    WOLF BLITZER
          We're not done with our
          potential to be better and
          learn what love really is.

Galen is surprised. He smiles and nods at
Blitzer.

                    GALEN
          Excellent.

Constantine squints at Galen. Galen returns
the gaze. He turns to the CNN stage and
gestures to someone.

Mother Fogelson is standing there with the other clerics. Galen gestures again and she's standing with him and Blitzer and Constantine.

                    GALEN (CONT'D)
          Mother. What do you think?

                    MOTHER FOGELSON
                  (off-guard)
          About the end of the world?

Galen smiles.

                    GALEN
          Yes.

She takes a long moment and seems to look within. She chokes up and tears brim in her eyes. She composes herself.

                    MOTHER FOGELSON
          I'm not ready...to give up.

Galen is intrigued.

                    GALEN
          "Give up."

                    MOTHER FOGELSON
          We're...better than this.

She points at the war destruction and debris around them.

                    GALEN
          What's keeping us from
          being better...than this.

He too gestures around them.

She looks at Constantine and Galen.

                    MOTHER FOGELSON
          Our...will. Our...Choice.

Constantine pales.

Michael, Inanna, the other enlightened beings appear in this spot, causing a ruckus among the TV production crews. Monitors show camera perspectives wildly re-composing, focusing, and steadying.

Sofia is near Galen.

Michael and Inanna step up to Constantine. He shrinks back.

                    INANNA
          You have gone beyond the
          pale.

They flank him.

                    MICHAEL
          You have imposed your will
          on others in a way that is
          contrary to the Universal
          Law.

                    INANNA
          Individual beings
          intertwined in personal
          struggles is one thing.
                    (pause)
          But you have usurped your
          role and created a false
          reality overlaid on the
          true reality.

Constantine whirls around desperately.

                    CONSTANTINE
          None of this matters.

He gestures (to the billions of dead throughout history).

                    CONSTANTINE (CONT'D)
          They all died and
          reunited...

He gestures to the sky, the Universe.

                    CONSTANTINE (CONT'D)
          Why do you care?

Inanna steps forward and puts her hand on
his shoulder. He freezes, either from fear
or physically.

                    INANNA
          It was not YOUR SAY.

Constantine looks around desperately.

                    CONSTANTINE
          But...

                    MICHAEL
          You've transgressed against
          Harmony.

                    CONSTANTINE
          Harmony?

                    MICHAEL
          All things are possible.

                    INANNA
          Not all things are
          beneficial.

Michael steps forward and puts his hand on
Constantine's other shoulder.

                    INANNA & MICHAEL
          You will cease to cause
          disharmony.

A bright blue hole opens up in the sky.
Everyone glances up at it, some unsure if
this is yet another calamity.

A cascade of opalescent energy, a
"waterfall" or an escalator streams down
to where Michael and Inanna are holding
Constantine.

                         CONSTANTINE
              No. Stop. Don't. You can't.
              Nooo. Stop! I am allowed...

He gets swooped into the opalescent
escalator to the sky and disappears.

Everyone is agape, except for the 10 other
enlightened beings.

EXT. SPACE

Venus, the second planet from the Sun, is
being licked by solar flares as the now
larger Sun is reaching it. Then it sucks
back its energy.

In several faltering but quick phases, the
Sun shrinks back away from Venus, then
away from Mercury.

Mercury glimmers as its feeble atmosphere
returns.

EXT. NEGEB DESERT

Galen looks around. Sofia does too.

The ENLIGHTENED BEINGS converge in a
tighter circle.

Wolf Blitzer and all of his global
colleagues focus their cameras and
microphones on this assembly. They point
to figures recognized from ancient human
stories such as the Anunnaki, Nommo, the
Feathered Serpent, and Elohim.

Michael, Inanna, Enki and the rest encircle
Galen.

He looks up to them.

                         MICHAEL
              Thank you.

                    GALEN
          "Thank you?" What did I
          do?

Michael smiles at Sofia and then at
Inanna. Inanna returns the smile and
shares it with the others.

Michael looks at Galen, stretching his arms
out in emphasis.

                    MICHAEL
          You...learned.

                    INANNA
          And you acted...

Galen becomes emotional. He looks at Sofia
and sheds tears, sobbing.

                    GALEN
          I'm not worthy--

                    INANNA
              (interrupting)
          All are worthy.

She puts a firm hand on his shoulder that
surprises him and snaps him out of his
self-pity; it may even hurt a bit.

                    MICHAEL
          You took the path.

Galen realizes what they're saying. He
nods, smiles, and looks up at them.

                    INANNA
          Taking the path proved it;
          if you need proof.

                    MICHAEL
          Holiness is not being
          better or more moral, as
          your culture has made it.
                    (MORE)

> MICHAEL (CONT'D)
> (pause)
> Holiness, being Divine,
> means being in touch with
> the fact that all is ONE.
> The more you remember
> that, the more Whole you
> are.

He winks at using the pun.

Michael and Inanna lean forward. As they do, their heads merge as their left hands do too and reach out to Galen's chin. They lean in and give Galen a long kiss.

That kiss becomes a bright glowing star that explodes in a flurry of sparklers. Galen is absorbed into that kiss, shrinking and inverting and then expanding into another side.

Galen, more of an amorphous body with only his eyes retaining their form, seems to be sucked into a wormhole, a black hole, that makes him enormously huge and able to see an enormous amount of the universe.

The twelve enlightened beings move away from Galen as he sees other bright orbs of energy, other enlightened beings take their places in the centers of galaxies.

Galen is knocked backwards as Michael, Inanna, Enki and the rest disappear.

The various news crews caught all of the terrestrial stuff on video.

Galen turns to Sofia and embraces her and kisses her.

MONTAGE AROUND THE WORLD.

The sun looks bright but normal.

The sky is a gorgeous blue. In a city

somewhere in the world people look up in wonder and joy. A YOUNG MAN shades his eyes and tears stream from his face. He can see.

THE ARCTIC CIRCLE The ice caps have congealed again, forming.

New York, London, and Tokyo are revealed as the flood waters no only recede but any damage seems to undo itself.

THE SAHARA, LIBYA People come out from their structures as a light rain falls. Livestock emerge and reunite with their stewards.

BRITISH COLUMBIA Forests heal themselves as burnt and blackened trees rejuvenate into lush green canopies.

OBSERVATORY Astronomers and astrophysicists watch data streaming into their computers.

                    ASTRONOMER 1
          I'll be damned.

The rest of the astronomers standing by collectively gulp.

Astronomer 1 looks up, realizing what he said.

                    ASTRONOMER 1 (CONT'D)
          Sorry.

HOSPITAL ROOM Trayvon turns from the window and joins a tired Allie, who is on her side with their brand-new baby swaddled expertly by one of the nurses. Trayvon kisses Allie's forehead and then his child's forehead.

He holds his hands together to his forehead in a gesture of gratitude. End MONTAGE

EXT. CITY - DAY

The world is gorgeous. People are moving
about. There are trains instead of cars
and delivery vehicles and a few smaller
vehicles.

People all seem content or happy. It's
not fireworks and giggles but there are
no homeless. No one looks miserable or
stressed out.

The buildings and structures all look
artful and kept up. Huge art projects dot
the surroundings. Construction is underway.

Galen and Sofia are in a plaza that
overlooks a lot of the city.

Sofia steps forward and gazes upon the
world with a huge smile on her face and
her eyes on fire with joy.

Jessica, Angelica, and Wilson, no longer in
a wheelchair or in ragged clothes, are all
there gazing at the beautiful world.

Sofia turns to Galen.

                    SOFIA
          Is this real?

Galen starts to speak and then catches on.
She winks at him.

He smiles at her and at the new world.

                    THE END

If you'd like to support our projects,
please visit our Patreon page at:
https://www.patreon.com/albinopiggorilla

To learn more about our projects,
please visit the AlbinoPigGorilla Studio website at:
https://www.albinopiggorilla.com